AFTERMATH

AFTERMATH

a novel by

Paul M. Pruitt, Sr.

QUID PRO BOOKS

New Orleans, Louisiana

Published in 2019 by Quid Pro Books.

ISBN 978-1-61027-398-5 (pbk.)
ISBN 978-1-61027-400-5 (cloth)
ISBN 978-1-61027-399-2 (ebk.)

QUID PRO BOOKS
Quid Pro, LLC
5860 Citrus Blvd., suite D
New Orleans, Louisiana 70123
www.quidprobooks.com

qp

Publisher's Cataloging-in-Publication

Pruitt, Paul M., Sr. — (1919–2008).
    Aftermath / Paul M. Pruitt, Sr.
        p. cm.
    ISBN 978-1-61027-398-5 (paperback)

1. Alabama—Fiction. 2. Twentieth Century—Fiction. 3. Trials (murder)—Alabama. 4. Women murderers—Fiction. I. Title.

PS3553 .H456 P7 2019

Original artwork and cover provided by Mary Ruth Pruitt, © 2019, used by permission. Author photograph on back cover inset provided courtesy of Paul M. Pruitt, Jr. Additional editorial consulting was generously provided by Lee Scheingold.

*To my three granddaughters, Juliet P. Barrett,
Meghan Marie Pruitt, and Mary Ruth Pruitt,
and in memory of my wife Ruth Rogers Pruitt.*

Foreword

In much of literature, a fine line exists between reality and fantasy. When we read or hear stories, the mental images we create can stay with us for a lifetime. Those images become our reality, whether the story was fiction or not.

Such was the case for me when my father, Paul M. Pruitt, Sr., told my brother and me bedtime stories whose characters were named Peahead and Lardtub. I have no idea where my father got those names. Like the stories themselves, I imagine that he made them up on the spur of the moment. In my mind, the setting for those stories was the farmhouse where my father grew up in Cherokee County, Alabama, near a crossroads called Gaylesville. Grandmother Mary Jane Pruitt lived on this property until the early sixties. As youngsters, my brother Paul and I loved to visit her and traipse over the property looking for arrowheads. Near the house was a big old barn with car tags from the twenties and thirties nailed to the walls, a huge oak tree planted by my grandfather George circa 1900, and the foundations of a covered bridge under which ran a beautiful creek where one always had to be wary of Cottonmouths. The remnants of an unpaved road leading to the bridge ran perhaps fifty feet from the front porch of the house.

When my father told us those very fictional bedtime stories, these images were always the reality in my head.

Thus was born the Pruitt family contribution to the Southern oral tradition. In the early '90s I told my own versions of Peahead and Lardtub to my daughter Meghan. The stories were different (I made them up as I went along), but the setting was again that beautiful country in Cherokee County. In my stories, the covered bridge was still there and often had a litter of kittens taking shelter there. My daughter loves cats.

Round two of Peahead and Lardtub was not to be the last time that Cherokee County occupied a place in my mind's eye. About 2005, my father began work on a novel inspired by his childhood friendship with a Confederate veteran who lived down the road. This veteran of the Civil War passed away circa 1930 when my father was about 11. Dad finished his work a few weeks before his death in 2008. I read it soon after, and once again the farmhouse, the barn, the covered bridge and the creek came alive in my mind. My father had passed on to us several memories of his conversations with the veteran. Some I recognized as I read the book, but the secret held for years by my father's protagonists was unknown to me. I was left wondering just how much of the story was inspired by this veteran's life or was based on actual events.

Many times I have wanted to ask my father, "Dad, did all this really happen?" Perhaps he would tell me to ask Peahead or Lardtub; they just might know.

Shannon Rogers Pruitt
Highland, Maryland

AFTERMATH

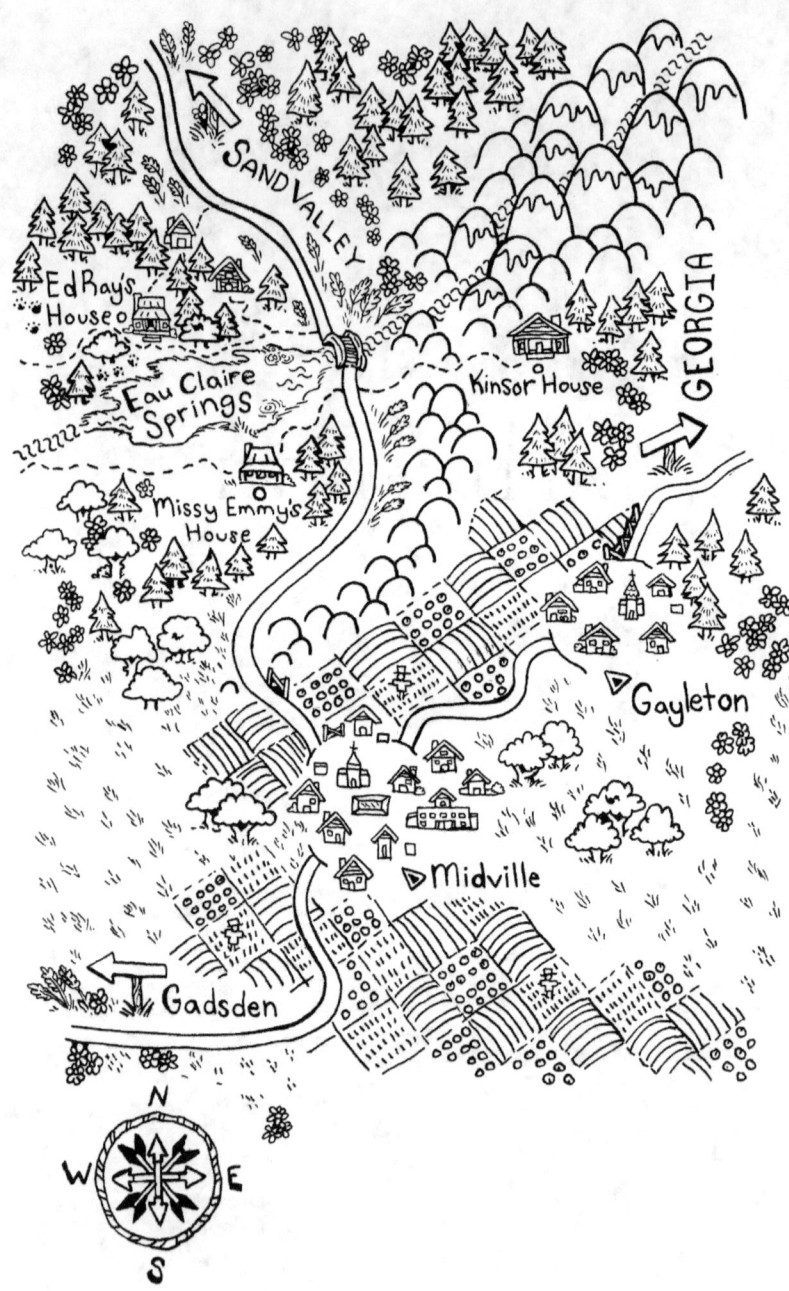

1
Appomattox and Later

That day in April was not like all other days. There were a multitude of differences, some of them obvious, some unexpected. Men and material were everywhere, and segregated into two sides. On one side, arms were stacked in haphazard rows; on the other side arms were borne by individual soldiers. This day marked the final muster of the Army of Northern Virginia.

For the Southerners, it was a mixture of emotions ranging from relief to bitter disappointment. They had fought so long and so hard to preserve their homeland. They were so loyal to their general that the thought of surrender seemed unreal—even disgraceful.

For the members of both armies there was one common expression. It was the blank, white-eyed stare of the combat veteran. It is a facial expression which warriors have worn since clans fought clans and tribes raided tribes in the dim past. It is an expression devoid of emotion. It is the expression of men who have had an empirical course in human anatomy, having witnessed body parts strewn upon fields of battle. It is the expression of men who have seen the worst, and who are no longer moved by further experience. Seeing comrades and the enemy slaughtered is so commonplace that it evokes a complete loss of sensitivity to horror. It is the universal coping mechanism that enables one human to take another's life, and most of the soldiers present at Appomattox Courthouse—men who had survived the fights at Petersburg—wore, or had worn, that same expression. James Polk Kinsor wore that expression, as did his brother-like friend, Alfred Courtney.

Kinsor and Courtney first met just prior to the Gettysburg battle, where they were both assigned to regimental headquarters as scouts, an occupation that carried with it a short life expectancy. Both had been injured during the engagements, though neither injury was at first considered serious. Courtney's wound, a shrapnel puncture of his right arm, soon healed. But Kinsor's wound, a bullet puncture of the left leg below the knee, proved to be very serious. His injuries had restricted blood circulation to the calf and foot. The result was gangrene, a most dangerous condition which, if not treated, is usually fatal. Field surgeons were preparing to amputate the leg, but he—cocking a small Colt pistol pulled from a pocket of his tunic—said, between gasping breaths, "I don't mean to be ungrateful, Doc, but you'd best not put that saw to my leg."

J.P. Kinsor was stubborn, and he survived; but as an annoyed surgeon had warned him at the time, his leg was severely ulcerated from the knee down and would remain so, possibly for the rest of his life. At first he could move around with the aid of crutches he had fashioned from the forks of small trees. He was able to rejoin his regiment during the trench warfare around Petersburg. Recently he had pushed his strength to the limit during the army's dash to Appomattox.

Foot soldiers and junior officers were unaware of what was then transpiring during the gentlemanly conference being held between

Generals Lee and Grant. As is the case in all armies, the private is the last to learn of command decisions and the first to die as a result of those decisions. So most conversations among the Confederate soldiers concerned questions about what was to happen next.

Throughout the long, dreary day, soldiers of both sides milled about, their clothing damp from the occasional drizzle. There was little taunting of each other, other than an occasional Rebel yell from some over-zealous Southerner. To the relief of all, an atmosphere of quiet was prevalent.

The two friends, Kinsor and Courtney, talked about their future plans. They had already decided that when the war was over, J.P. would accompany Courtney home to spend a few days together and to allow him to recuperate as much as possible before he undertook the return trip home. They had talked about the things they would do, neither knowing of conditions at their homes. Their ancestral backgrounds were diverse, even divergent. Courtney came from an affluent family of Southside Virginia planters, slaveholders. Kinsor came from a yeoman farm family from the ridges of North Alabama. He was an only child, who at best could expect to inherit a three-room house and one hundred hillside acres of land. But they shared an ambition to return to their homes and to resume the lives they had known before the war.

After numerous rumors and the passage of two days, the official results of the conference between the two commanders were announced. The news which most concerned the two friends was that they were paroled and could return to their homes. Alfred Courtney had anticipated that some such announcement would be made and had sent his man-servant and protector, Nate, home to get horses to ride home. Two days later he was bitterly disappointed when Nate returned with one mule. Nate reported that the plantation had lost every horse to foragers from both armies, and that the mule was one of three that had been successfully hidden from the raiders.

"What about the old folks?" asked Alfred. "Old Marse and Ma'am are fine," said Nate. "They're lookin' forward to seein' you—an' that a right smart." "How about the people?" said Alfred. "People still in their cabins," was the response. "They been told they're free, an' that made 'em happy. But they got no partic'lar place to go. They got no plowstock, so nothin' much to do 'cept work in their truck patches." Nate and Alfred chatted on for a while about their old home-place. They had been together as master and servant since they were toddlers. They did not discuss Nate's freedom—it probably didn't yet occur to Alfred that Nate might ever want to leave him.

Alfred and J.P. received their written paroles and departed Appomattox, passing through Farmville, then south to the Courtney plantation. Somewhat to Kinsor's embarrassment, he rode the mule while Courtney and Nate walked alongside. Their arrival was welcomed by Courtney's parents and his sister; an older brother had been killed at First Manassas. The conditions existing on the plantation were much as Nate had described. For the moment, most of the slaves had remained. Neither Union cavalry nor Confederate raiders had seen fit to burn any of the buildings, though they had taken livestock and many objects of value. Apart from the buildings, fields and woodlands, three mules were all that remained to serve a human community of forty-odd souls.

Both young men were jubilantly received at the Courtney home. Ma'am Courtney was especially solicitous of Kinsor's ulcerated leg. She prepared a huge poultice of slippery elm bark and carefully swathed the lower leg and foot with it and with boiled cloth from a worn-out sheet. This treatment eased the pain sufficiently to allow Kinsor to get a few hours of restful sleep.

If J.P. had had his way, he would have started home soon after his arrival at the Courtney home. He had heard nothing from his parents for more than a year. Being an only child, he was anxious to get home to care for them in their old age. But Ma'am Courtney would hear nothing but that he stay there to regain his strength. Consequently, he did not start home until the first week in June.

As Kinsor prepared for the long trip home, he realized his wounded leg might not permit him to travel on foot. He was much touched by the generosity of the Courtney family's gift of the mule he had ridden from Appomattox. In spite of his protests that the Courtneys needed the mule more than he did, Marse and Ma'am Courtney left no doubt that he would take the mule. So at dawn of a June morning, he packed his spare clothes into saddlebags that had belonged to Alfred's older brother, and in which he found rations for several days. These included bread and fruit from Ma'am Courtney's kitchen and a store of hardtack that had been given to J.P. and Alfred by Union soldiers. "You're welcome to it—better you than me," said Alfred, shaking J.P.'s hand.

"And here's something else that might come in handy," said Nate, his deep voice coming over the saddlebag on the mule's off side. J.P. thanked Nate; preoccupied, he didn't ask what it was. That night he found that Nate's "something" was J.P.'s pocket Colt, well-oiled and wrapped in cloth, with a handful of loads in a small tin. He had surrendered the pistol with his musket at Appomattox. He wondered whether he'd ever get the chance to ask Nate how in the world he had managed to rescue it.

Mounting the mule J.P. departed, bearing at first southwest. So much of Virginia had been foraged and pillaged by both armies that there was almost no food available for man or beast. Kinsor had at first planned to return home through the Piedmont area of the Carolinas and Georgia, but further thought told him that he could expect a cold welcome from people of those areas because they had no material means with which to extend hospitality. Even if they had food to sell, Confederate money was now worthless. So he guided his mule toward the less-foraged mountains of Appalachia. The population of the mountains traditionally had little of the world's wealth; but what they had they were willing to share.

A normal day's travel by muleback would have been fifteen to twenty miles, and if Kinsor had traveled that distance each day, seven days a week, he would have arrived home during the first week of July. He had begun the journey with a good supply of food given him by Ma'am Courtney. But there was little they could give him to feed the mule. Consequently, he had to pause at regular intervals to allow the mule to graze on whatever plant growth was available. For that reason alone, the most progress he could expect was fifteen miles per day.

Added to that necessary delay was the problem of the wounded leg. The motion of the mule would at times cause excruciating pain; so serious was the pain that Kinsor would be forced to stop the mule and let some of the pain subside. Thus, after five days of torturous travel, he arrived in the mountains. So far he had spent nights on the ground, wrapped in a quilt given him by the Courtneys. By day he used the folded quilt as a makeshift pad for this wounded leg.

As he made his way toward home, he was rarely able to get nourishing feed for the mule. Although the mountain people were hospitable, they had little to share with the stream of Confederate soldiers who, like Kinsor, were going south and west to their homes. Most of them were walking, some suffering from old wounds. Many of the families along this mountain route had lost family members or close relatives in the war. They were sympathetic to all, but they had little to share. As best they could, they would invite as many as they could accommodate to sleep in their homes. Because of this most appreciated hospitality, Kinsor spent many nights in the homes of kind strangers, wrapped in his quilt and lying on the floor. As he slept, his mule was tethered outside in an area of weeds and grass; not an ideal ration for an animal that was carrying a man fifteen miles per day. Work animals need grain in their feed, but the mountain people had no grain to spare. They were subsistence farmers, and their hillside fields yielded little. Years of erosion, lack of fertilizer, and poor soil management had worn down the land. There was little ground suitable for farming left in the mountains.

So day after tortuous day, Kinsor made his way homeward. He lost weight, mainly from poor nutrition. His mule also lost weight for the same reason. There were times when he would feel faint and be forced to stop and try to regain his strength. At those times, he doubted his ability to endure long enough to reach home. On several occasions he because delirious from fever. He experienced flashbacks of the horror of battle; sometimes he considered suicide. Then he would feel ashamed that he had ever thought about killing himself. Above all, the thought of his parents and home preserved his determination to stay the course. But that was easier said than done. Each agonizing day saw him lose strength to a combination of poor diet, constant pain, and loss of sleep. Again and again, he wondered if he would survive to get home.

Finally, on the eighteenth day of July, Kinsor emerged from the mountains into the Appalachian foothills. This was familiar territory: it was the land of his birth. Ranges of low-lying hills replaced steep mountainous peaks. Kinsor's spirits were somewhat revived. The mule could navigate the hills with greater ease; there was much more grazing for him. Now the prospect of home and parents raised the horizon of J.P.'s life to a brighter level.

Kinsor was never certain of his location during the return home, but now he could estimate with some degree of accuracy how much farther he had to travel. So, as he tethered the mule on the evening of the eighteenth of July, he told himself he would reach home in three or four days. As he prepared a bed of leaves at the foot of an oak tree and wrapped his lank body in his quilt, his outlook gradually brightened. As usual, his sleep was more from exhaustion; fitful rather than sound; and filled with weird dreams.

At dawn came the raucous calls of a family of blue jays. They were relentlessly attacking a red tailed hawk; the hawk was less than happy that his early morning search for breakfast was so rudely interrupted. Kinsor waited and listened as the drama unfolded. A thought came to him that he and the hawk had something in common. The hawk was denied the privilege of an easy hunt by the pesky birds, while he was denied a normal life by a leg wound that could never heal.

Today was the nineteenth of July 1865. Both the mule and rider were somewhat relieved to find their progress less difficult than had been true since their entry into the mountains. Then Kinsor began to be aware of subtle changes in the terrain—changes that suggested mass damage from the recent past. Of course, he was seeing the scars left by the passage of two armies. This was the result of the preparation for General Sherman's infamous "March to the Sea." As Kinsor crossed into north Georgia, the intensity of damage increased until the earth looked as if a giant storm had swept a path across the land. Farmland was lying idle for want of work animals. The population of the area had been composed entirely of yeoman farmers and small storekeepers. And they had been foraged by both armies until nothing of use remained. In many instances foraging was abandoned: looting, pillaging, and worse things took its place. Some families even lost cooking utensils, and there were many families whose homes were burned simply because the looters found nothing to loot. This was a face of war that Kinsor had heard rumors about but had not seen. He had begun seeing the devastation as he approached Chatsworth and when he arrived at Calhoun, he saw the worst damage. But after Rome the damage was scarcely noticeable. He spent the night of July 22 at Coosa, where a strong spring of water poured from the bank along the road. A wood-framed church gave him protection from a rainstorm just after midnight.

He was now familiar with his surroundings. As dawn of July 23 broke, he ate the last of a pone of cornbread. A housewife on the western outskirts of Rome had given him what was left of the cornbread she had made for her family. His joints were stiff from sleeping on the hard floor of the church, and he had difficulty mounting the mule. He led the mule alongside the doorsteps in order to gain the advantage of height, and swung up more easily.

At nightfall he had progressed to another church, repeating the events of the previous night, except that there was no rainstorm. He'd had nothing to eat all day and was weak from pain and hunger. He located an old and rusty bucket, filled it with water, and used his next-to-last match to start a fire. From under an oak tree he gathered a large quantity of acorns. For an hour Kinsor boiled the acorns; then with fresh water he repeated the process. He then peeled the tough outer hulls from the acorns, and after another session of boiling, he emptied the bucket of water and spread the acorns on a flier—which advertised a service of prayer on behalf of the Confederacy. After a few minutes, he began eating the acorns. When he had enough, he gave the remainder to the mule.

Daybreak found him mounted on the mule and laboriously wending homeward. He had traveled this road many times as a youth, and he passed several homes whose occupants he could faintly remember. He did not pause for his usual noon respite, hoping to reach home by nightfall. But sadly that ambition had to be abandoned because by mid-afternoon his leg was so painful and the mule so jaded, he was forced to spend the late afternoon and night in the barn of a deserted farmstead. His sleep was at best fitful and at worst nonexistent. He was so filled with the anticipation of reuniting with his parents and of resuming his former life that he was unable to rest his body from the rigors of the trek from Appomattox. As best he could remember, he was less than five miles from home.

Kinsor arose in the pre-dawn darkness of July 24, mounted the mule, and began the last leg of his tortured journey. At about eight o'clock he was on the outskirts of Midville. The people of the town, the county seat of Chufenee County, were going about their daily routines. They paid little notice of the lone rider and his jaded mule, for returning soldiers had become a common sight. As he approached the courthouse square, he met a few acquaintances from his youth. They were friendly, but they were not particularly elated to see him. Most of them were ex-soldiers themselves; some of these had lost a leg, or arm, or eye.

His progress through the town was necessarily slow, giving him a chance to observe and absorb the atmosphere that pervaded the place, one that would continue to exist for a generation to come. As he began to leave Midville and travel north, he was sobered by the seeming indifference of the townspeople he had encountered. Finally, as he rounded a bend in the hillside road, he could see the landmark of his youth, Eau Claire Springs. At the sight, a wave of nostalgia overcame him and a tear cascaded from each eye. He was home! He was home! All the toughness of four years of war was momentarily melted from his being and he was again a carefree boy innocent of the horrors of war. He hoped—how he hoped—that he would never have to turn his hand to violence again! So deep were his emotions that he was unaware of his painful leg, nor of his bone-deep weariness.

When he arrived at the springs, he dismounted and lay down and buried his face in the sparkling water. The mule likewise drank deeply and noisily. Then Kinsor remembered that farther around the springs a huge bed of watercress grew. He was ravenously hungry, so he ate a large handful of the succulent weed. He offered some to the mule, who was not very fond of plant's pungent flavor.

As he was about to remount and continue home, he was startled by a weak, low moan from near where he was standing. At first he could not determine the direction from which the moan came, when a repetition of the sound directed his attention to a clump of bushes along the bank of the spring. Kinsor approached the bushes and was astounded to see a small human form lying on the ground. The face, head, and reddish blond hair were matted with dried blood. Kinsor could see that the person was still breathing. Checking one slim wrist, he saw that the young person had a faint pulse. As he examined the body more closely, it became evidence that the victim was female and fair-skinned. Her face was severely distorted, discolored, and swollen to the point where she could not be recognized.

J.P. pondered what to do, but not for long. His own home was not far away—indeed, it was a quarter mile east of the Eau Claire oaks—but he knew that he must somehow get her to Emmaline Clifton, the community midwife, herbal practitioner, and substitute physician. So he laboriously lifted the comatose girl and, by painful straining, placed her across the back of the mule. Thus he transported her a mile down the road to the home of the lady better known simply as Miss Emmy. The exertion in lifting the girl onto the mule and in the painful walk from the springs to Miss Emmy's house had so exhausted him that he was forced to sit on the ground. Otherwise, he might have fainted.

There was no sign of anyone at the house. But after a few loud "hellos" the front door opened, revealing a woman of uncertain age. She crossed the porch, descended the steps, and approached the huddled group in the yard.

"We need help, Miss Emmy," was all Kinsor could say.

"Who are you?" asked Miss Emmy. Then, in recognition, she exclaimed: "Oh, my God! J.P.!"

"Yes, Ma'am, I am, but this girl needs help more than me."

"Who is she?" asked Miss Emmy.

"I don't know. I found her at the springs and brought her here to you."

Miss Emmy was accustomed to lifting and moving persons who were too weak and too ill to move themselves. So she gingerly removed the still unconscious girl from the mule's back, grasped her in a firefighter's carry, and took her inside her house. She placed the girl on an iron cot in the enclosed dogtrot of the house. She brought soap and hot water and gently bathed the girl's face, removing as much caked blood as possible. She then used clean warm water to remove matted blood from her hair. That the girl was near death was obvious. Her pulse was rapid, but very weak. Her breathing was shallow and slow. Her skin was pale and cool.

"I'm afraid we've a hopeless case," said Miss Emmy. She then looked at Kinsor, a long look which scanned his entire body.

"You're evidently not much better off than this girl. What's wrong with you?"

Kinsor then related his experience of a bullet wound and its sequel.

"Lemme see that leg," ordered Miss Emmy.

Kinsor lifted his pants leg to expose the bad leg.

"Lord, have mercy! You need to rest en' let me do what I can to heal your leg," was the response.

"Not now, Miss Emmy. I must go on home. I haven't seen Mamma and Papa since 1862, and I have had no word from them in over a year."

"Oh, then you don't know. Both your parents are dead. Your daddy died of the pneumonia in January 1863; your mamma caught it from him en' died a month later."

Kinsor was struck dumb at hearing this news. He sat on the edge of the cot and wept. His body shook and trembled with anguished sobs as his mind tried to comprehend the enormity of his loss. He had to ask himself what further evil had been prepared for him by the gods of fate, and, of course, he had no answer.

He stood, taking his make-shift crutches in hand, and made his exhausted way to the front porch, down the steps, and to the end of the graveled walkway. Here he sat in the shade of an ancient mulberry tree and continued to sob. A mockingbird trilled her medley of calls, music which failed to penetrate the aura of sorrow surrounding Kinsor. He felt that truly he had nothing to live for. He was uncertain if he wanted to continue the short distance to his home. At long last, and he did not know how long, he was momentarily interrupted in his grieving by Miss Emmy's voice.

"J.P., you mustn't let this ruin your life. I know you en' your parents was very close—you have my sympathy. But you are still a young man, although an exhausted and sick one. You need rest, relief from pain. You mought not ever be whole agin'; but you can better the life you have left. I know if you go to the old Kinsor place, the memories will ride right over you. So you can stay here with me 'til you are stronger. You can help me care for that girl, who may not be able to survive the beatin' she's received. Now, come in the house, bathe en' shave. Thet will improve your feelin's. You can use my daddy's razor.

2
Medical Arts

So began a prolonged period of convalescence for both the unknown girl and for Kinsor. Miss Emmy was widely known for her talents as a midwife and practitioner of herbal medicine. Her treatment was essentially the same for both of them. Slippery elm poultices, pain killing drugs, and wholesome food. By careful experimentation, Miss Emmy learned that, although the girl was nearly comatose, she would accept food which was pureed almost to a liquid state and allowed to trickle between cheek and teeth.

It was a tedious but effective process, and it sustained life. Miss Emmy was also a firm believer in controlling pain, and she administered just enough laudanum to allow her patients to get restful sleep. She had a supply of a patent medicine, Dr. Hendricks's Golden Medical Discovery, which contained twenty percent alcohol and one-half percent laudanum. The girl needed no pain-killer, but Kinsor often suffered from his wounded leg. Through trial and error, Miss Emmy learned that a tablespoon of the medicine taken every four hours would relieve the pain enough to allow Kinsor to sleep restfully.

Thus began a life-long system of medication which would permit Kinsor an existence of tolerance. That his leg might never get "right" was painfully evident. There were times when he thought of amputation—then firmly put the thought away.

July faded into August, with its dog days, humidity, and heat. Strength seeped ever so slowly back into Kinsor's body, with a slight improvement in his physical abilities. He was able to assist Miss Emmy in caring for the girl. He began to regain the lost weight. A healthy glow returned to his skin. He reluctantly accepted his condition and settled into a routine of limited activity. His curiosity concerning the injured girl gave him a motive to assist Miss Emmy in her nursing.

Lacking any other identification, they referred to the young woman simply as "the girl." Her care had to be intensive and constant. To avoid bed sores, her position had to be changed almost by the hour. Her bandages required frequent changes. Her personal hygiene was a duty of Miss Emmy's; the lifting and moving of her body were the duties assumed by Kinsor. Throughout late July and August the girl lingered on the edge of life and death. There were days when her breathing was so irregular and shallow that Kinsor and Miss Emmy despaired of her prospects for life. Poor blood circulation to her face caused the horrid swelling and discoloration to linger. For weeks her only speech was a series of weak moans.

Looking at the girl's face, the fact was that a broken jawbone had positioned her chin to the right of center. Miss Emmy had fashioned a long cloth rag into a makeshift sling. It extended under her chin and up and around her head to give limited support to the fractured jaw. It did not, however, realign the chin. The result—if she survived—would be that the bones would slowly knit together and the chin position would become permanent. If she survived! That was a frequent subject of talk between Miss Emmy and Kinsor. The roller-coaster status of the girl's condition gave them cause both for hope and despair.

The days and weeks passed. Kinsor could never garner enough courage to visit his home. He suffered flashbacks of his war experiences, and in spite of Miss Emmy's ministrations, his leg would erupt in pain. His suffering was intense, so much so that Miss Emmy, at times, urged him to see a surgeon and have it amputated. He adamantly refused, citing soldiers he had heard of whose limbs, long gone, continued to throb with phantom pain. Perhaps he was superstitious enough to think perhaps he had exhausted his allotment of luck in surviving the war. Such reasoning demonstrates the ability of the human mind to rationalize any idea or position. His choice would set the dimensions of the remainder of his existence.

3

First Recoveries

That the girl survived was a miracle. At intervals during the long weeks of that fall, she would open her eyes; eyes that were apparently unseeing and without recognition of her surroundings. This event kindled some hope in her caretakers that maybe she would live. But with that hope also came the cold fear that, if she did live, she would be little better than a living corpse.

But the miracle continued, for eventually the eyes opened and the wounded mouth also; and she uttered the word "water!" The astounded caretakers hurriedly provided a glass of water, and raising her head, carefully let water from the glass trickle into her mouth. Miss Emmy and J.P. were cautiously optimistic to witness what they both considered a wonder. It was a testimonial to the intense care given by them, especially by Miss Emmy.

As for J.P. Kinsor, his condition was little changed. He was constantly depressed, often in pain, and he was easily exhausted. He could not bring himself to go to his parents' home. Increasingly, he spent his time alone. He had no friends, nor did he want friends. He was isolated, preferring to dwell upon his not-to-be forgotten memories of home; ghosts of a world that he could not rejoin. Frequently, in laudanum-induced dreams, he returned to the horrors of war. In those dreams he again witnessed the mangled bodies of his comrades; he heard the pitiful screams of the dying; and he offered water from his canteen to the feverish lips of the wounded. To all intents and purposes he was now fighting another kind of war. His wounded body and ravished nervous system were having revenge for the damage the war had inflicted. This was a war without lines of demarcation—and though he would live to a very old age, he could never win it.

Some days he would hobble the several hundred yards from Miss Emmy's house to the springs. On his first visit, he was both surprised and pleased that, as he sat at the water's edge, several brook trout had stared at him from the crystal clear water. While they were not tame, neither were they wild. They were accustomed to being fed by visitors to the springs, a fact Kinsor had known since childhood when he fed them himself. After that first visit, he would take a chunk of Miss Emmy's cornbread and slowly toss small bits into the water. That became a ritual, repeated almost daily as weather permitted. It was a ritual which allowed him momentarily to escape all that his life had become. He childishly thought of the fish as his only friends.

He became so obsessed with the ritual of sitting and staring into the clear water that he could not experience respite from his miseries anywhere else. Only at the springs could he view his existence with any semblance of optimism.

Miss Emmy was aware of his condition. She was also aware of another problem which was equally as serious. She had suspected for several weeks that the girl might be pregnant. She was now positive. The girl's abdomen had developed the tell-tale growing lump which is positive evidence of an expected child. Kinsor had not noticed the change, but when Miss Emmy remarked that the girl was pregnant, he looked with amazement at the outline of the girl's body under the sheet.

"We may lose her yet," Miss Emmy remarked. Then she punctuated that remark by adding, "I don't see how her body can withstand the awful strain of a pregnancy en' the delivery of a child." She had assisted the local doctor in so many childbirths that she knew a woman's body should be in the best of condition in order to survive the growth and delivery of a child.

The girl's pregnancy caused a temporary respite for Kinsor's preoccupation with his own condition. He was unsure if he should continue to live at Miss Emmy's house, and he was equally unsure if he could bear to live alone in his dead parents' home. He was becoming more nervous about his ability to survive. In fact, he often wondered if he wanted to survive. He was aware of his condition, but lacked the neurological stability to form rational decisions. He finally realized that he was depending on Miss Emmy to decide for him.

Thus it was that in February of 1866, Miss Emmy confronted Kinsor. She had been aware for some time of his deteriorating state of mind, and was determined to do what she could to start him back to as normal a condition as possible.

"J.P., I know you have experienced the horrors of war. That's wounded you both physically en' in your mind. I understand why you are angry, bitter. Anyone would be! You have faced your military enemy with courage en' honor. But you are no longer facing the Yankees; the enemy now is yourself. You have two choices: you can refuse to recognize that fact—and do nothing but pity yourself. Or you can face up to the real facts of your life. Those facts are that your leg will always be more or less painful; also that you won't escape the war's damage to your nerves. An old friend of mine lived by a sort of saying. No matter how bad things got, he would say to himself, 'Nevertheless, I'm goin' on.' If you are the man I think you are, you need to adopt that same attitude."

Kinsor was silent, dreadfully silent for several seconds. His gaze was fixed, unseeing on the floor in front of him. His lips quivered. Tears coursed down his cheeks. His shoulders trembled and at last a sob escaped his chest. Then great heaving sobs sprang from his mouth. He sat on a chair and continued to cry for several minutes. Slowly, ever so slowly, the crying subsided and he sat motionless, still staring at the floor.

Throughout the entire episode, Miss Emmy had observed him with critical eyes. Finally, she stated: "You needed that, I reckon."

Without a word, he picked up his crutches and left the house. He hobbled aimlessly in the yard for several minutes. Finally, he found himself on the well-worn path to the springs. Once at the springs, he sat in silence, his eyes staring sightlessly into the crystal clear water. The trout swam by and stared as only fish can stare, expecting the accustomed hand-out of bread crumbs. So deep was Kinsor's dolor that he did not see them. His thoughts were irrational. He had never been this low during the most dangerous and painful phase of his gangrene infection. Then he had had the hope that at some time the war would be over, so he could return home to his parents. He could care for them as they became old and unable to care for themselves. Perhaps he would marry and rear children of his own. Those were reasonable and normal hopes; hopes shared by many of his comrades. He had returned to find his parents dead. His physical and emotional states erased any hope he might have to rear a family. His very birthright had been usurped by the fates. He no longer felt in control of his existence. In his mind, it all added up to his life being without purpose or usefulness. He decided to end it all.

But how? He considered the choices: poison, drowning, a gunshot to the head. Poison and drowning were too slow and messy. A gunshot would be swift and almost painless. And there would be no problem. His colt was still in his saddlebags; he took it out, checked reflexively that it was loaded, and put it in his hip pocket. Yes, now he had a way to exit the horrors of this life.

He arose and hobbled slowly, but with determination, toward his childhood home. As he approached the homestead, he was not surprised at the condition of the yard. Weeds of many varieties had grown waist-high all around the house. The doorsteps to the dog-trot were rotted and sagging. As he opened the door to the left, he was almost overcome by the musty odor, the overhanging morass of cobwebs. There was his father's favorite chair, the fireplace with ancient ashes and charred pieces of firewood. There was his parents' bed with its over-stuffed feather mattress. Over the ancient chest of drawers was a small portrait of his grandmother. There was the door to his room, and over there, the door to the kitchen.

He opened the kitchen door and stood looking. Everything was as he remembered: the cupboard, the dining table, the wood-burning cookstove with his mother's gallon-sized distillery sitting on top. The stovewood box had several sticks of wood in it. And there in the center of the oil cloth-covered dining table was the familiar cluster of dishes: a sugar bowl, salt and pepper shakers, a pepper sauce cruet, and a glass urn containing several teaspoons. Yes, how could he ever forget his mother's kitchen?

He turned from the kitchen door and walked to the door of his bedroom. He hesitated as he touched the doorknob. His hand felt heavy, almost refusing the twist of the wrist which would open the door. He felt as if he would suffocate, so emotional was he. Finally the door opened, revealing the oh-so-familiar contents of the room. His bed with its fat feather mattress, covered with his mother's handiwork—a tufted counterpane containing the traditional peacock figure. The old wooden shipping crate which served as his footlocker. The kerosene lamp on the side table by the bed, the source of light by which he had read his few precious books. The armoire in which his old clothes still hung. The cane-bottomed chair in which he had so often sat. The now-empty gun rack above the door which had always supported his shotgun and rifle. He wondered what had happened to the shotgun, and supposed someone had stolen it after his parents had died. The rifle he had carried with him when he enlisted in the Army. It was lost the day he was wounded at Gettysburg.

There was nothing else to see. He sat in his old chair. His body slumped. Suddenly he was very tired. He stared vacant-eyed at the plank floor. He could not control his thoughts. They seemed to run in all directions, resulting in conflicting emotions which rendered him unable to act or think rationally.

He then did the only thing possible under such circumstances— he wept. Self-pity so engulfed him that he was forced to surrender his very being to those circumstances. He could conceive of no future, no past. Only the present seemed real, but it was useless. He was useless and without purpose.

He did not know how long he sat there among the mementos of his lost youth and innocence. Finally his sobbing ceased; he was left with the empty feeling that nothing mattered, that the fates had decreed that his value as a human was now reduced to zero. He remembered his original reason for being there—reached back, and pulled his revolver from his trousers. He went to his father's chair. He sat there, thinking dully of the time when Nate had said "it might come in handy." For what seemed like a long time, he stared at the weapon in his lap, unable to act. Then he was startled to hear the voice of Miss Emmy; he returned the Colt back to his back pocket.

"I thought you might finally come here," she said, coming into the room. "I'm glad. Now that you're better, you need to see this old house in order to finally and truly realize that nothing will ever be the same as you left it four years ago. What you have done today can be the first step to reclaiming your life. I had worried you might come here to kill yourself, which would, of course, have been a cowardly act. But you're no coward, J.P. Kinsor! Yes, death might ease your pain—but it would deprive the girl and me of help and support, support which we desperately need if the girl is to survive childbirth. Oh, yes, you *are* needed! Now, git up en' come with me. We have work to do."

4
Interiors and Exteriors

The candor with which Miss Emmy had spoken seemed harsh, even mean, to Kinsor. War-hardened as he was, oddly he could not comprehend the real intent behind the tongue-lashing she had given him. But the life she had accepted, after it had been almost thrust upon her, demanded a pragmatic approach. She had shunned marriage in order to care for her sickly parents. The experience gained in nursing them had hardened her outlook—had turned her, though she was less than thirty years old, into an imposing woman of no particular age. For Miss Emmy, the facts of life were real and must be confronted face to face. She was a realist. What she had said to Kinsor was her way of expressing concern and restoring his confidence.

As Kinsor sat there in his father's old chair, staring at the ancient ashes and the charred wood, he suddenly felt very empty, the emptiness one feels when very hungry. Except that the empty feeling extended to his mind. He felt purged of his bitterness and sorrow. The extended periods of sobbing, plus the words of Miss

Emmy, had perhaps allowed him to rid himself of his self-pity.

How long he sat there in a sort of trance he did not know. He began to revel in what he could only call a feeling of freedom, a freedom of spirit, not freedom from pain or debility. Those would be with him to his grave. But by God's grace, he would rise above it all and be worth something!

At long last he gathered his crutches, closed all the doors to his old home, and hobbled his way back to Miss Emmy's house.

As he entered the house, his thoughts turned to the girl. Prior to this time he had considered her only as an unknown and unknowable individual, a person without personality, without a known past. As he entered the room where she lay, he looked upon the outline of her body on the bed. For the first time he saw the blonde hair, the large blue eyes, the fair skin. He was startled at her condition. He saw the outline of the increasing distortion of her body, the effects of the fetus growing inside her. He saw the terrible scarring and misalignment of her facial structure. And he was suddenly ashamed, ashamed that he had been so engulfed in his own condition that he had given little or no thought to just how terrible her wounds had been, nor to what a miracle had transpired by her survival. And he was reminded of what selflessness and devotion Miss Emmy had demonstrated. His shame increased as he compared the conduct of the two women to his own. He resolved then and there that his avowal to be worth something was to be his motivation. He would somehow learn to endure the painful leg. Miss Emmy was correct in telling him that he was never going to be whole again, and nothing he or she could do would make it any different.

Over time, the human animal is wonderfully adaptive. Over time, the human brain can be conditioned to ignore pain. Over time, a stressful, painful existence becomes normal. And while pain may never go away, it becomes a normal part of living and it thus becomes bearable. When it becomes bearable, the human can function in a productive manner. This adaptation assumes a patient, strong-willed person. J.P. Kinsor had a strong will and he would learn patience from Miss Emmy.

Emmaline Clifton was an unusual person in many ways. Uneducated as she was, her intellect was amazing. During the mid-nineteenth century, education was considered a luxury and was not an aid to the yeoman farmer who lived by subsistence farming. Enough schooling to learn to cipher and to do rudimentary writing was enough for boys. Girls required even less. Girls were expected to marry, have children, perform household duties, and in their spare time, help the family in growing crops.

Miss Emmy, whether by design or by fate, escaped that life of mostly drudgery by being a voracious reader and by never marrying. She chose rather to first care for her ailing parents and after they were gone, to care for those in the community who were ill. She borrowed books on childbirth from local physicians. She observed physicians as they delivered babies. She absorbed medical information as a sponge absorbs water. She learned the symptoms and treatment of pneumonia, of pellagra, of malaria, and of septicemia. Her presence in a sickroom seemed to give the patient a confidence and strength of will to recover. One physician remarked, "Miss Emmy is as competent at delivering a child as any doctor in the area."

She, of course, had to charge for her services, for that was all she did. But she was often paid in farm produce. During Reconstruction, "hard" money was especially scarce. Yet she never refused a family's request for help, and she never insisted on payment. There were families who were so deep in poverty that they never paid her.

Her main source of pride came from the children she delivered.

Her great sorrow was the birth of stillborns. Miscarriages were commonplace. Mothers died from "blood poison" soon after giving birth. Ignorance of the practice of hygiene cost the lives of thousands of young mothers and their babies. The life expectancy of a child born in the mid- and late-nineteenth centuries was, at best, somewhere in the fifth decade.

Miss Emmy's continued scolding and encouraging of J.P. Kinsor resulted in a gradual but certain improvement in his attitude. Ever so slowly he learned to accept his condition and to look outside himself. Thinking over the girl's wounds, he often felt ashamed that he had ever complained. He worried about the girl and her coming crisis, and he wondered why he worried. After all the horrors he had witnessed on the battlefield, how and why could he have tender feelings for anyone? Prior to the war, he had been an affectionate, loving son to his parents and had had an interest in several young women. But he did not know, and had no real interest in finding, any eligible young women now. So this feeling toward the girl was new and also a bit puzzling to him.

So it was, on a day well into that long autumn season that the girl had asked for water. From then on her progress was much accelerated. She could move her arms and legs, she could adjust her position in bed; and she could form simple sentences. Miss Emmy was much encouraged. On Saint Valentine's Day in 1866, she asked the girl if she remembered her name. After a long interval of time in which her brow furrowed and tears formed in her eyes, she replied, "Cynthia."

"What is your last name?" asked Miss Emmy.

After another period of searching her memory, she said, "I dunno."

It was at that moment that her identity changed from simply "the girl" to the more familiar "Cynthia." Now she was no longer an enigma. She became a personality. She was knowable. And to Kinsor she was somehow appealing—her situation touched whatever residue of human compassion remained in his psyche. Or so he thought. What he was really feeling, although he was not aware of it at the time, was an incipient renewal of that indefinable attraction between a man and a woman. The attraction in this instance was not an erotic one. Rather, it was the more beautifully tender feeling which eventually produces a bond that endures for a lifetime. Her first glimmer of a smile thrilled him deeply.

All this renewal of his real self was somehow confusing to him. In an effort to sort it all out, he visited his fish friends at the springs. As he tossed bread crumbs into the sparkling water, he closely watched the competition of the fish as they swam to the bread. The winning fish would break the surface as it grabbed the bread, then dart away to a safe distance to swallow it whole. He envied their freedom and energy. Yet they were not really free, for they were confined to their watery world just as he was a prisoner of his world. This reminded him of a series of experiences from his youth.

In back of his old home on a steep hillside was a rocky outcrop. When he first found the cliff, he was twelve years old and was not as keenly observant. A year or so later, he found himself examining the cliff with a more discovering eye. Where before he had seen nothing but scree and decaying leaves, he now saw the subtle signs of wildlife. Wild animals leave few signs of their presence, especially around their dens. But as he looked carefully at the total scene, he had seen little trails among the scree—leading to the base of the cliff and then into it. He kneeled to one knee to look closer. He now was certain that some animal or animals called this home. His gaze settled on a lone hair sticking to the edge of a rock. He carefully grasped the hair and examined it closely. He saw the tell-tale multi-color of the raccoon. And at that instant he heard the slightest suggestion of a noise at the base of the cliff. He looked up in time to catch a momentary glimpse of a masked face. He had discovered the den of a clan of raccoons!

Among wild animals, raccoons are notorious for their intelligence, cunning, and courage. They are protective to an extreme when threatened. Many a dog has had his ears, nose, and lips slashed by the teeth and claws of an angry raccoon. J.P. was at once fascinated at his discovery and determined to get better acquainted with his sly observer. Later he revisited the den with ears of corn in his pockets. Weeks had passed without another glimpse of the inhabitants of the cliff. He would sit silently, expectantly awaiting some activity, and when there was none, he would leave the corn on a large rock. Invariably the corn was gone when he next visited.

Finally, and after numerous trips to the cliff, he was rewarded with a thrilling sight. At first he thought he was hearing the chirping of a distant bird, but then he heard a slight sound of rustling leaves. First there was one tiny marked face peering at him; then there were two; and finally three baby raccoons were peering at him as if to ask: "Who are you?" J.P. sat very still. An observer would have had difficulty in deciding who was more curious—J.P. or the baby 'coons. Being so absorbed in watching them, he was unaware of time passing. He had already placed the usual ears of corn on the flat rock and was thrilled to see one of the babies carefully advance toward the rock, all the while carefully watching J.P. The other two babies soon followed, but the first—larger and marked with a white spot on one ear, was clearly the leader. The ears of corn being too heavy to carry, they proceeded to feast on them there on the rock. A slight movement at the base of the cliff revealed the face of the babies' mother. She would occasionally call them, but they ignored her calls. Their leader, whom J.P. had christened "Titan" for his size and bold manner, seemed to have a mind of his own. Thereafter J.P returned whenever he had a moment away from his chores. Sometimes he would read quietly—from *The Boy's King Arthur* or an *Elson Reader*—while the young raccoons played around him.

This memory of his youthful encounters now stirred in him a desire to revisit the cliff. He had no idea whether the raccoons would still be there, but he hoped they would. His very existence seemed, in his confused state of mind, to depend on revisitation of experiences that were tender and natural. If they were still there, he wondered if they would remember him. So with the aid of his crutches, he limped toward the cliff. His progress was slowed by undergrowth and fallen trees, but at long last he found himself at the cliff. There was the flat rock where he had placed the corn; there were the tell-tale little paths leading to the base of the cliff; but not a sound nor a motion could he detect. He sat on the adjacent rock and waited—how long he knew not. After the passage of perhaps one-half hour, he was rewarded with the least suggestion of rustling leaves. His pulse quickened. At least something was living there. He gave a low whistle as he had done so many times in his youth. His whistle was answered by a high-pitched chirp, the unmistakable sound of a curious raccoon. Again a low whistle was answered by a chirp. Then to J.P. a wonder occurred. A masked face cautiously peered from a crevice, and above the mask was an ear bearing a white spot! This was the face of a huge, grown-up Titan!

The two sat curiously eyeing each other for a long time—neither of them moving or making a sound. Titan's piercing eyes stared through a black mask at J.P. Soon caution overcame curiosity and Titan retreated into the crevice, leaving J.P. amazed and elated. He was certain his old friend had recognized him! Another piece of his life had thus been restored. He felt better.

5

Newborn

The spring season of 1866 seemed to erupt rather than to ease into being. In a period of one week, latent buds burst into leaves and blooms. The temperature, which had been unusually cold, was suddenly mild and soothing. Somehow nature seemed more alive than usual. As March progressed from blustery winds to warm breezes, the progress of Cynthia's recovery increased. Her distorted body was a grotesque exaggeration of her youthful figure. For a long time, she had only been able to sit on the edge of the bed. Then she was able to make one or two faltering steps from the bed to a rocking chair. As she sat in the chair, Miss Emmy demanded that she rock back and forth. The gentle exercise of rocking would aid in restoring muscle tone and strength. By the ides of March, she was able to get from the bed to the chair with just the least help from her caretakers.

Cynthia's powers of speech lagged behind her physical recovery. She was unable, or unwilling, to remember her surname, or any other item of identification. At first, she could utter single words.

She was unable to put words into a series. She was essentially an infant learning the very rudiments of speech. Ever so gradually did she gain enough verbal skills to speak in very short, simple sentences. Every word was a learning experience until late in March when she asked Miss Emmy why her body was so distorted. When she was told that she was going to have a baby, tears welled up in her eyes, and her face mirrored the fear she felt inside. She looked at Miss Emmy with a pleading, helpless expression. At that instant the infant in her womb changed position, kicking downward and causing Cynthia to grimace in pain.

Miss Emmy looked at Cynthia for several seconds, and then said: "You have been so brave throughout your ordeal—you must not give up now. A child will be an awesome responsibility, but I'll take care of you until you're fully recovered. Perhaps the child will prove a blessing to you, but you must first love it. You must love it in spite of the treatment you have had from your attacker. The child is the result of your being raped, not the cause. So try your best to be happy at the prospect of being a mother."

So it was in the pre-dawn of March 27 that Miss Emmy and J.P. were awakened by a loud scream from Cynthia. They were both at her bedside in an instant to see a face contorted with pain and a body stiffened with tension. She had experienced the first contractions of labor. As the pain subsided, her facial expression changed to one of fear.

Miss Emmy was at once absorbed by the task at hand. She was a veteran at attending childbirths, having delivered most of the children in the area. She instructed J.P. to start a fire in the kitchen stove and to rekindle the coals in the living room fireplace. She also instructed him to draw water from the well and begin heating it on the stove.

While he was occupied with those tasks, Miss Emmy examined

Cynthia to determine the extent of dilation. There was little dilation, so a long wait was in store for all of them.

Cynthia's progress was excruciatingly slow. Her contractions were sporadic, coming at intervals ranging from twenty to thirty minutes, a fact which was of much concern to Miss Emmy. She thought they should be spaced with some regularity.

As is true of most first-time mothers, dilation was slow and very painful. Cynthia complained of a severe backache, a fact that pleased Miss Emmy for she knew it was a normal companion of childbirth. Hours passed with slow progress. By noon she was twenty percent dilated, and the contractions were somewhat more regular and evenly spaced. Anesthesia was unknown, and even if it had been known, none was available. Miss Emmy knew that laudanum, taken in the quantities necessary to control the pain, could easily harm or kill the baby. So contraction after painful contraction came and went with Cynthia suffering through each.

Miss Emmy had instructed Kinsor to massage Cynthia's back during contractions. Of course it did little to relieve the misery, but it gave Kinsor something to occupy his time during the long wait. Little conversation occurred, only that which was necessary to care for the distressed Cynthia. By twilight Cynthia was visibly exhausted. Little fretful moans escaped her mouth, moans which grated on Kinsor's nerves to the extent that he asked Miss Emmy in private if Cynthia was going to die. Being assured that the process was almost normal and that, no, she was not going to die, Kinsor returned to massaging her back.

Just before dawn on the twenty-eighth of March, a piercing scream brought both Miss Emmy and Kinsor to Cynthia's bedside. Her body was rigid, her face was flushed, and her eyes bulged as an intense and prolonged contraction occupied her entire being. After examining the progress of the birth process, Miss Emmy instructed

Kinsor to bring towels and boiled water to the bedside.

"The baby is about to be born. Yo're no longer needed here, but you can keep a supply of hot water and towels as needed. Go and set by the fire 'til I call for you."

Sitting by the glowing fire, Kinsor experienced a mixture of emotions. He was not the father of the child, but he felt a strong paternal attachment. He had no part in the conception of this child, yet he felt that he was somehow involved. He realized that Cynthia was innocent of any wrong-doing. Yet he knew the stigma of an illegitimate child would cast its shadow on her and on her child from now on. That the child could never know its father aroused an odd anger in Kinsor. What a gross injustice to an innocent mother and child! He was helpless to do anything about it.

Shortly after five a.m. on the twenty-eighth of March, a long, animal-like scream brought Kinsor out of his frustrated anger. He could hear Miss Emmy urging Cynthia to "Push, push, push hard!" A final scream was followed by a few seconds of absolute silence. Kinsor wondered if Cynthia had died. This hiatus of silence was followed by a scream of an altogether different nature. This scream was tiny in comparison. It was a sound of protest. It was the primal sound of life. It was the sound of a newborn baby, suddenly thrust from the security of the womb into an environment which continually attacks and eventually conquers.

"You have a beautiful baby boy," was Miss Emmy's first remark to Cynthia. "You must now rest and regain your strength."

6
Nomenclature

Following the birth of the baby, Cynthia was listless from exhaustion. She showed little interest in her surroundings. Her scarred and distorted face was more or less expressionless. Her sole interest was the infant. That she had bonded with him and loved him was apparent. As she looked at him, her expression would visibly soften and a broken smile would appear.

Miss Emmy expressed the fear to Kinsor that Cynthia would sink into a case of "baby blues," the then-current reference to what later became known as postpartum depression. This meant little to Kinsor—he was so perplexed by his own emotions that he could not comprehend her. The injustice of the situation still rankled him, and that he could understand. But his feelings of responsibility to Cynthia and to the infant, he did not understand. In reality, he knew he could not be blamed for the rape and injury to Cynthia. Nor could he be blamed that the baby could never know his father. But he had the feeling that he somehow had a vested interest in both of them. That was what he could not understand. Rescuing

Cynthia from certain death was what anyone might have done, he thought. Helping nurse her back to her present state of recovery was also what he should have done. All those feelings, intermixed with the emotional wreckage resulting from his war experiences, rendered him incapable of thinking rationally and clearly.

The advantage of youth soon enabled Cynthia to recover from the rigors of childbirth. She was again able to leave her bed. In spite of Miss Emmy's objection, she ventured into the yard in mid-April with the infant in her arms, and she sat under an early-budding mulberry tree. With mild, sunshiny weather she was comfortable, and after the long months of convalescence she felt exhilarated. Her vision roamed the horizon, absorbing the beauty and the freshness of nature in spring. She looked at the sleeping infant, as yet un-named. That she had not yet chosen a name for her baby was a source of irritation to Miss Emmy. But even Emmy had to admit to herself that namelessness was only one of this baby's troubles. Most illegitimate children grew up knowing their father's name—this one probably would never know. And what child, of whatever birth, was likely to be raised without knowing its mother's maiden name? Miss Emmy liked to keep things tidy, including family trees; but this was a messy situation!

As Cynthia sat in the shade of the mulberry tree, as she looked into the face of her child, her thoughts were also drawn to the need for a name. Her mental processes remained slightly rusty, so she spent an hour or so trying desperately to choose a fitting name. Finally she thought of the feminine names of the months of the year. April, May, and June were common names for girls. What was the most masculine month? She thought of March and August. August had no special meaning for her, but her little fellow had been born in March! Yes, that would be his name!

Just then Kinsor returned from one of his frequent visits to the springs. He sat beside Cynthia and made small talk about her being outdoors and about how nice the weather had turned.

Then she told him her choice for the name of her baby. Kinsor agreed that the name was an apt one. He then asked her what surname the baby would have.

"I dunno. If I can't remember my own family's name, so how can I say what his full name will be?" came the tearful reply from Cynthia.

"Then give him my name, if you like," said Kinsor.

Thus, the product of a vicious rape became March Kinsor.

7
Declaration

The improvement of Cynthia's physical health was paralleled by a continued improvement in J.P.'s emotional health. He began to show an interest in things outside himself, especially in Cynthia and March. He had volunteered the use of his name, he had helped nurse Cynthia from the brink of death, and he had aided Miss Emmy during the birth of the baby. Consequently, he felt that he held a certain vested interest in both of them. A nagging worry loomed larger and larger: How could Cynthia live and rear a child? A long time must elapse before she could perform any work, even if there was work for her to do. Rearing March would be all she could expect to do for at least a year. That he was genuinely fond of Cynthia, J.P. had no doubt. That he felt a paternal attraction for March was beyond doubt.

In late April the three of them were sitting under the mulberry tree in Miss Emmy's front yard. Miss Emmy was away at a neighbor's house delivering a baby so they had the place to themselves. There had been little conversation, but J.P. felt the time had come to ask Cynthia what she planned to do when she was fully recovered. Her reply was an outburst of tears—tears of fear and frustration.

"I dunno what I am to do! I dunno who I am; I've no family; I've no property; and I can't stay with Miss Emmy forever. She's been real good, real kind—and I can't thank her 'nuf."

J.P. was silent for a time before he replied to what Cynthia had said. His expression was one of thoughtfulness. Then as if he had been thinking about the dilemma for a long time, he turned to her and said: "You can move into my house."

She looked at him with some surprise and said: "Only if you'll live there too."

J.P. was momentarily stunned, unable to reply. Finally he blurted out: "But what will people think?"

"At this moment, I dun't care what they think. I'm worried about March! People can think whatever they may! I dun't care. My life can never be whatever it was before all this happened. You can't imagine how grateful I am to you and Miss Emmy. I only pray that I can repay you."

After this little soliloquy, tears welled up in Cynthia's eyes. She sobbed uncontrollably, the first time she had exhibited such emotion.

J.P. arose, went to her side, and placed his hand on her shoulder. Before he could utter a word, Cynthia stood and embraced him in a prolonged hug, all the while continuing to cry. He was unable to return the embrace for several seconds. At last he clasped her in his arms. Thus they stood, each unable to speak until finally Cynthia broke the awkward silence by saying, "J.P. Kinsor, I love you!"

8
Making a Start

Thus it was on that day in late April 1866 that their lives were joined in the dual efforts of surviving and in some way making a living. If either of them ever thought of marriage, no mention was made of it. That there was a bond of affection between them, there was no doubt.

Both sat in silence for some time. March was busy making baby sounds and aimlessly exercising his arms. He was a healthy, happy baby. He seldom cried and then only when he was hungry or needed a diaper change. J.P. got up and paced the yard, deep in thought. His thoughts so consumed his attention that he was unaware of the return of Miss Emmy. He was startled to hear her voice.

"I see you three are enjoying this beautiful spring day, but why th' expressions of gloom?"

Neither J.P. nor Cynthia answered her immediately, but finally J.P. replied: "We have been talking about our futures. Neither of us can see how we can survive on our efforts. Neither of us has a family for support, and we are both unable to work. I have the house and the forty acres of land, but I am unable to do farm work. Cynthia has March to care for. She can't do manual work."

"You're both welcome to live here with me as long as you need to. I have room to spare in my home, and the rent from my land will sustain us. So you should not worry about your futures for as long as you need to recover your health. I am proud of the three of you. But I have one question—do you plan to be married? If so, when?"

Cynthia looked at J.P., then dropped her gaze and remained silent. J.P. was also silent for a moment and then replied: "Evidently fate has decided that we should be together, and if that be true, it seems useless to think of marriage. If we live together for a certain period of time, the state will consider us legally married. And to answer your question, no, we haven't discussed it. However, I will leave that decision up to Cynthia."

Cynthia smiled at J.P., an admiring smile, an affectionate smile. Then she turned to Miss Emmy and said, "First of all, I can't never thank you 'nuf for what you've done for March and me. But for you, I'd most probably be dead, and certainly li'l March would not have been born. J.P. has given his name to March—he ought to get a medal for that! And then he's offered to share his home! We will have a house with furniture, a barn, tools, and the mule J.P. rode home. We can plant a truck patch this year and farm the forty acres next year. And we can live near you and be of service to you."

Cynthia's expression of gratitude and love broke through Miss Emmy's practiced detachment. Tears welled up in her eyes. She blinked and momentarily turned her face away from J.P. and Cynthia. But she quickly regained her composure and replied, "I have never had chi'ren of my own, and the Lord knows I have longed for them. You three are now my chi'ren. You owe me nothing more then what you have already given me in your love and affection. I shall forever be grateful to the gods of fate thet brought us together."

This brief scenario sealed a bond among them that was in a sense stronger than a real family bond. This bond was voluntary, not genetic. There was no inherited familial duty—just the natural result of the tragic and random circumstances of their collective struggle for survival.

Their problems were not unique. All citizens faced the awful aftermath of war; the devastation of the economy; the hated presence of Union troops of occupation; the dead and wounded fathers, brothers, cousins, uncles, and friends; and perhaps worst of all, the feeling of utter frustration and hopelessness which overwhelmed the entire population. Man's cruelty to his fellow humans is never so evident as when he goes to war.

That part of the South where J.P. grew up was never a slave-based culture. There were no holders of vast acreage, no palatial homes, and no elite class. Farms were small, just large enough to support a subsistence level of farming. Slave ownership had been unnecessary, and in any case was entirely out of the financial reach of those yeoman farmers.

None of those factors was of concern to J.P. and his adopted family. That they survived at all was the result of their ingenuity and Miss Emmy's support. Cynthia cleared the vegetable garden of weeds and brush and grew a late crop of vegetables. Miss Emmy furnished corn for grinding into meal. J.P. set traps for small animals for their meat. Cynthia became skilled at catching fish, although J.P. forbade her fishing in the springs.

Miss Emmy lent J.P. and Cynthia enough to purchase food staples for a year. In the meantime the mule, which had been given to J.P. by the Courtneys and which he had ridden home, had long since recovered from the starved condition of its arrival. They decided to call him Abel, an apt title because he was their first and only source of power. Eventually, Cynthia learned to plow; Abel was her willing partner. By the spring and summer of 1867, they were cultivating most of J.P.'s forty acres. With borrowed seeds and advice from neighbors, they raised vegetables, corns, and a little cotton. For several years, with occasional further assistance from Miss Emmy, they paid their taxes and kept out of the clutches of supply merchants. All they wanted was independence and a quiet life.

Isolated though they were, the couple did not avoid all contact with the outside world. Not long after his return J.P. wrote (with pen and paper supplied by Miss Emmy) a note to Alfred Courtney, thanking him for his friendship and his family for their generosity. Over the years the two men took to writing each other around the Christmas season. Their notes were brief, typically laconic, but through them Alfred learned about March's progress, Abel's usefulness, the situation of the crops, and the antics—mock heroic usually—of several stray dogs who had turned up at the Kinsor place and were indulged partly because they earned their keep, but mostly because each had shown an immediate and peculiar bond with Cynthia. Over the years Cynthia befriended a number of canines; by the times discussed below, her pack included B.J. the herd dog, ratters Lily, Ros, Ben, Bonnie, and Roby, guard dog Lady, and the music-voiced hounds Bingley, Margo, and Emma. Of Cynthia herself, J.P, wrote little—ashamed, perhaps, that a woman was working on the farm. He wrote about the hard times following the Panic of 1873; he wrote less about his physical ailments.

Alfred, for his part, disclosed that he had stayed on the family farm, weathering the economic and political troubles of the times. He had never married—as J.P. knew, Alfred's fiancé had died of measles during the war. Instead he devoted himself to caring for his parents and for the land. Once he had adjusted to the idea of Nate's freedom, Alfred had not tried to hold him back. He assisted Nate in getting an education from Hampton Institute, a newly formed school in the Tidewater. "He already knew how to read, write, and cypher," Alfred wrote J.P., adding that Nate had "learned while sitting quietly, just inside the door of our tutor's classroom."

At Hampton, Nate polished his grammar, learned to be a teacher, and for several years he kept a country school near Farmville. In one of his letters Alfred mentioned that Nate, in addition to his studies, was learning the trade of barbering—much in demand among the residents, white or black, of crossroads villages in the Southside. Indeed when he wasn't teaching, Nate would pack up his barber's kit and indulge in a penchant for seeing the country—a holdover, perhaps, from his army days, certainly one of the simple delights of freedom. Polite and self-effacing, he had little difficulty in securing short-term barbering posts at hamlets on or near the railroad lines, sometimes at a surprising distance from home. Eventually as his skills matured, Nate traded in the underpaid struggle that was teaching for the bay rum pleasures of the tonsorial art.

9

Interlude: Transitions

The remaining years of Reconstruction were indeed a long struggle for J.P., Cynthia, and March. As was true of their neighbors, every day they found some obstacle to overcome. Accustomed as they were to subsistence farming, they were able to do just that—subsist. As the years passed, they were burdened less by the residual bitterness of Unionists and Secessionists. More troublesome were such mundane matters as the lack of a stable currency or any reliable network of roads. Perhaps worst of all was the lingering sense of defeat which darkened the thoughts of the entire white population.

To add to the general misery, the "panic" year of 1873 brought in its wake such low crop returns that J.P. and Cynthia were hard-pressed to provide clothes and other necessities. With no other option, Cynthia spent much of her time hand-sewing their clothes, especially for the rapidly growing March. J.P. did what he could to help with family chores, but being limited by the leg wound, he was often forced into relative idleness. He purchased a second-hand shotgun, twelve-gauge, rabbit-eared, and spent as much time as he could hunting in the nearby woods, often helped by two or three of Cynthia's dogs. For several months of the year, wild game was their only source of meat. During such times squirrel stew was a frequent dish on the table. The couple had little if any knowledge of dietary needs; so they had no inkling that the squirrels, fed on a diet composed mainly of acorns, in turn nourished them with a fair source of niacin.

The lingering effects of Cynthia's injuries made her voice often little more than a whisper, so it fell to J.P. to tell March goodnight stories. J.P. filled March's head with stories of two mischievous brothers named Peahead and Lardtub and the adventures they had as they visited their Uncle Ebenezer and Aunt Saphronie. With J.P.'s soothing voice, March was most often asleep long before J.P. needed to invent an ending. He avoided telling March tales of the war, especially at bedtime. But sometimes, as the days trooped past, he would mention things he had seen and people he had known. At such times he told about men and women who had met their troubles and preserved an unconquerable humanity. Alfred Courtney and his guardian angel Nate figured more than once in J.P.'s recollections of the unvanquished.

As the years passed, Cynthia became more skilled in farm work. She bargained for and bought another mule to join the faithful Abel. She was thus able to utilize the full forty acres they owned. She grew cotton, corn, and hay in addition to the vegetable garden. In their self-sufficiency they barely noticed the economic crisis of 1893, a year that was long remembered and discussed by people in the neighborhood. That year was the wettest within memory of the oldest old-timers. Field crops could not be cultivated; thus, they were overgrown by grass and weeds, rendering a yield far less than normal. J.P. and his family tightened their belts a bit, but managed to pay their taxes and avoid the trap of debt.

J.P. and Cynthia seldom ventured into Midville. At first, J.P. had wanted to avoid the sight of a blue uniform. He was still occasionally subject to flashbacks and nightmares in which he relived the horrors of his army experiences. In those nightmares, he could hear the din of battle, the screams of the wounded and dying. He would see his comrades killed; he would see an enemy soldier fall when he knew he had fired the bullet that had hit him; he would awaken in a cold sweat, sitting upright in bed; and he would pace the floor in his peculiar limp until he could regain his composure. These involuntary recollections would continue to torture his dreams for the rest of his life.

Cynthia's life centered around two full-time jobs: raising March and keeping up a wearying round of farm work. To J.P. she seemed a tower of strength, full of tenderness for their little boy but ruthlessly efficient in kitchen, barn, and fields. For outside work—indeed, for most occasions—she adopted the poke bonnet, whose long brim, almost a beak, shielded her fact from the sun. Around people, even her family, she kept her eyes down so that no one could see her face.

The little family was so involved in their struggle to survive that events outside their neighborhood seldom attracted their attention. It mattered not that Grover Cleveland, a Democrat, was to serve as president (twice!). To the Kinsors during these years, it mattered little who was the county sheriff; or probate judge; or who pastored the local churches. By 1890 March had grown into a handsome young man who was able to help Cynthia with the farm work and the cutting and stacking of a winter's supply of wood for the fireplace and kitchen stove. And as the new century neared, they were able to look with hope for an improved set of living conditions. Even the war with Spain, which changed the map of the world, launched the political star of Theodore Roosevelt and made the United States an imperial power, raised scarcely any dust on the Kinsor place—or truth to tell, among most of their neighbors.

March Kinsor might have wanted to march off to war in the summer of 1898, if he had not had better things to do. By that time March was already married to Daisy Burkhalter, a young woman from the neighborhood. By the outbreak of that "splendid little war," they were planning a move to Texas, like so many other young people from the Deep South. Indeed by the turn of the century, March and Daisy were settled in on a farm not far from Texarkana, and had made J.P. and Cynthia grandparents several times over. They exchanged postcards regularly with the old folks and with Miss Emmy, all of whom spent long evenings discussing their news. Their move to Texas was a journey into a new country, a new century, and so is not a part of this tale. This story must go onward toward a place where, as a Mississippi writer would later put it, the past wasn't dead—it wasn't even past.

10

Remembrances of Things Past

O n several occasions J.P. had been invited to attend the annual meeting of the Confederate veterans in the area. He
had never felt the need to attend a meeting where the day's
menu would include nothing but stories of individual experiences
during the war. He had spent so much time and energy in his recovery from his own experiences that he had no desire to relive
them at a meeting. But because of the insistence and friendship of
Elwin DeJohn, once a sergeant in his regiment (now the probate
judge of the county), he agreed to attend the meeting in August
1900.

The meeting was held in the sanctuary of the Campground
Methodist Church, so named because it had been a training site for
raw recruits entering the Confederate Army. Today the church was
packed with veterans, their families, and white citizens in general—
these reunions were thought to be notable public gatherings.

J.P. was surprised at the number of veterans in attendance, most
of whom, like himself, had been wounded to some extent or anoth-

er. Some had lost legs; some had lost arms; some had lost both; some were blind. His friend Sergeant DeJohn had lost a leg and could walk awkwardly on a crude peg leg. At the sight of those survivors, J.P. was humbled to think that his own wound, although painful and serious, was insignificant when compared to those he saw that day. While his first conception of the event had been a negative one, he now felt a comradeship with these men who had fought so valiantly in defense (as they viewed it) of their homelands.

The meeting agenda was a simple one and typical for that period in the South. The first item was an oration by Ezekiel Vanderhooven, headmaster of the local academy and a recognized and admired speaker at various functions. Oratory was a much admired skill, and Zeke, as he was affectionately known, was a master at oration. His physique was remindful of Ichabod Crane, with flaming red hair and a complexion mottled with large freckles. His dress, which never varied, was a white linen suit, a white shirt, and a black string tie. The outfit was topped off with a broad-brimmed white hat.

Zeke's topic was, quite naturally, the War of the Confederacy. He extolled the many virtues of the men who had fought for so long and so bravely. He extolled the virtues of the cause for which they fought. He extolled the courage and determination of the survivors. He especially praised the valor and sacrifice of those who were slain and whose remains were in unmarked graves all over the South. His speech lasted for an hour and fifteen minutes, but to his audience, it seemed much shorter. In common with successful speakers, his presentation was spell-binding. As he neared the end of his speech, his voice reached a crescendo.

He ended his presentation with a short but dramatic prayer, an invocation of a divine providence on the heroic survivors of a most horrible war. Then he spoke to the audience: "As you leave here today, my plea is that you will embrace these valiant men to your hearts, that you will respect them for what they have accomplished, and that you will give whatever aid and succor you can to their waning lives. By their deeds they have demonstrated the epitome of true manhood; they responded to the call to duty; they gave their full devotion in our behalf. Our past is ever with us; the present is past tomorrow; our future is unknown and unknowable. Also let us forever remember and honor those who paid the extreme price and whose bodies now lie moldering in lonely graves from Vicksburg to Gettysburg. This is my message to you today, a message I fervently hope you will accept and that will cause you to pause often to pay homage to these brave survivors of the Confederacy."

Zeke's speech was, of course, the main attraction on the agenda. The audience sang several songs which were popular during the great conflict, the most popular being the marching song, *Tenting Tonight on the Old Camp Grounds*. The singing of the old song brought tears to the eyes of several veterans. Troops traditionally sing as they march. The first tribe to invade the space of a neighboring tribe must have sung some sort of marching song.

As for J.P. Kinsor, the meeting caused him to remember the long marches he had suffered through. His mind flashed back especially to the retreat from Gettysburg on his recently wounded leg. He remembered the diet of roasted corn he was forced to eat when rations were short or nonexistent. He remembered the discomfort of too little clothing on bitter, windswept days. He remembered the soreness and stiffness of his body after a night spent sleeping on the ground in rain-soaked clothing. He remembered the friends and comrades whose tragic deaths he had witnessed. The screams of the wounded and dying seemed to echo in his head and in his heart. Would he ever be able to remember his experiences without sinking into an abyss of depression? He returned home depressed, resolving never to attend another Old Soldiers Reunion. Yet every so often he would turn up at the Campground reunions, mostly from a desire to see once more the dwindling band, the brotherhood whose members shared the same thoughts and feelings that he—that they all— kept hidden inside.

11

Life Histories

As the new century unfolded, J.P. gradually became less of a recluse, while Cynthia remained withdrawn, seldom appearing outside their home and always hidden behind an elaborately long poke bonnet. She had little to do or say to anyone except her husband and the aging but still active Miss Emmy. She was a good cook, often preparing food in novel and unusual ways. Also, she had learned to distill corn whiskey using J.P.'s mother's stovetop still. In fact, she gained a local reputation as a maker of fine corn whiskey—the best made in the vicinity of the Springs.

The still had only a small capacity. Its product, at first, was purchased by neighbors who, if they could never quite penetrate the shadow cast by the poke bonnet, instinctively trusted this reticent woman. As times improved and her reputation grew, travelers on the Midville Road occasionally stopped to purchase her wares.

She, for her part, grew less apprehensive about meeting her customers; and, far from shrinking from such encounters, she began to study the men whose purchases provided a useful addition to her household income. She was an efficient manager of that small income, as she demonstrated by bartering home-grown products for food staples from peddlers whose "rolling stores" passed by her house on weekly schedules. Peddlers are talkative by choice and by vocation; as the years rolled by, Cynthia listened to their tales of births, marriages, illness and deaths. Unassertively, she encouraged their gossip; and by the end of the old century's last decade, she came to know a great deal of the goings-on in the countryside.

J.P. was no social gadfly, but he did emerge from his isolation occasionally. His friend Elwin DeJohn, the judge of probate for the county, would sometimes visit the Kinsor home. The two of them as they sat and talked were a relaxing picture of two aging men who deeply respected each other. They never discussed the war, their wounds, or their feelings about their experiences. Judge DeJohn was ever the up-beat optimist, the hail-fellow-well-met; the consummate politician who knew every registered voter in the county by first name and family size. A one-legged Confederate veteran, he was unbeaten after his first election, which had taken place shortly after the Union troops were withdrawn. He rarely encountered opposition in subsequent elections. He enjoyed his status as an elder statesman and humanitarian. As time passed he sensed that his friend needed some social exercise to help alleviate his moodiness, his tendency to dwell on the violent and hopeless past. Often he asked J.P. to visit him in town, and on several occasions he suggested that J.P. would be a welcome visitor at a new club, a group of independent inquirers that had been meeting in town since Theodore Roosevelt's election—a group of men and women, said DeJohn, who would take him out of himself. For a long time J.P. resisted these overtures; but on a June day in 1905, some business in Midville coincided with a club day, and he let DeJohn carry him along.

So it was on that summer day that J.P. first went with Judge DeJohn to a meeting of the Sagacious Sophomore Society. The Triple S Club, as it was called, was not really an organization. It had no membership roster; it had no constitution; it had no by-laws; it had no agenda for meetings; it kept no records of meetings; it had no purpose except to engage in civil conversation. And even conversation was not a requisite—a member was welcome to just sit and listen. The meeting times were erratic, occurring most often on each fifth Saturday evening at the spacious home of attorney Ambrose McKye. The only strict requirement was that each attendee would notify the club's hostess—Mrs. Christina Dobbs, widowed sister of lawyer McKye—not later than the Thursday preceding the fifth Saturday. A home-cooked meal was served by Miss Crissy at each meeting; her culinary standards were of the highest order, and her cook Delnora was locally famous. On most fifth Saturday evenings there were as many as ten attendees. To McKye, whose wife had died in 1897 and whose only son was away at the state law school, a full house was a mighty pleasant thing. J.P. soon came to know all of the frequent attenders by sight; with several he quickly developed feelings of camaraderie and esteem.

One of J.P.'s long-time acquaintances was his neighbor Edward Elroy Raye, a self-educated genius and, like J.P., something of a social recluse. Raye was a voracious reader with multiple interests and an impressive vocabulary—it was understood among Triple-S members that the club owed its alliterative name to one of his verbal eruptions. A substantial landowner whose farm included Eau Claire Springs and all the surrounding area, he cultivated just enough acreage to provide a subsistence life. He had divided the land surrounding the springs into pie-shaped sections. He would not sell the title to any of those sections; rather, he had leased several of them to persons he considered good stewards of nature.

Each lessee paid rent of a few dollars per year—enough to cover the taxes with a little left over—payable on January first of each year. As Raye would often say, he did not own the land. Rather, he owned a legal document which gave him stewardship of the land.

Edward Raye was a resourceful person. He had rigged a tightwire from his front porch to the springs. From the wire was suspended a six-quart bucket. A windlass on the porch allowed the bucket to slide down the wire to the springs, retrieve a full bucket of water, and return it to the porch. Asked what prompted him to rig the device, he replied, "I am essentially a lazy person. Laziness is often the mother of invention." In physical appearance, Raye was tall and lanky. His hair, which had once been very dark, was now a salt-and-pepper gray, and it was far from tidy because he trimmed it himself, looking into his mother's hand-held mirror. His deep-set eyes were a piercing, steel blue; he looked at the world from under heavy brows. His facial expression was that of constant bemusement. Nothing seemed to surprise or shock him.

Had Raye lived in ancient Greece, he would have resembled Socrates more than Plato. He would have been an admirer of thoughtful, self-examined minds, but without writing about them. He would never have been a stoic. He admired oratory and those who were skilled orators. He was a great friend to Zeke Vanderhooven, and when he had the opportunity, he would go to the academy and listen to lessons as taught by Zeke. He was a collector of knowledge, by means of which he interpreted his relationship to nature and to the universe. A bachelor by inclination, he could never have loved a woman half so intensely as he loved words.

Another of J.P.'s new friends was his host, Ambrose McKye, the leading and most successful attorney in Midville. His regular attendance was only in part the result of his home being the meeting place of the Triple S Club. McKye being a widower and his sister Christa being a widow made their living in the same house not only a convenience, but—to their minds—a social necessity. The McKye ancestors had moved to Midville's vicinity from Virginia in the last decade of the eighteenth century. His father and grandfather were both lawyers, both having graduated in law from the University of Virginia. So it was only natural that Ambrose had attended the same institution. He had graduated with high honors and had briefly considered practicing law in Richmond or Alexandria or maybe Washington, D.C. But the attachment to family and the appeal of a simpler, slower-paced life overcame whatever desire he may have had for a more lucrative practice.

McKye soon learned that his choice of location had its consequences. He entered practice with his father and very early on learned what it meant to be a successful lawyer. His father was a perfectionist who felt insecure about any case which was not completely researched. He felt that he must know or accurately predict every issue that might be introduced at trial. He must know every question that might be raised by either side at trial, and the answer to each question. He always searched for novel approaches to legal issues, even though he had great respect for legal precedent.

To his chagrin, Ambrose had at first been allowed to handle only trivial matters. He wrote land deeds until he hoped never to see another title record book. He continued to research law books just as he had in law school. He analyzed wills, searching for ways to attack or defend a will, depending on whether he was representing a plaintiff or a defendant. In short, he was for a long time his father's junior partner.

Such was his father's example that Ambrose eventually appreciated his philosophy of legal practice. It was then that his father allowed him to enter the courtroom to litigate simple cases on his own. As time passed and as he gained confidence, he was amazed at the number of cases he won. He was proud that his preparation and analysis of cases were so often superior to the opposing counsel, the result being that over time he gained a reputation that, "If you are going to court, you should employ the McKye boy as your lawyer."

Physically, he was an imposing figure. He stood six feet tall; he weighed more than two hundred pounds; his hair was very dark brown; his eyes were greenish blue; he was not bald, but his hair was thin all over his head. He tended to perspire when others did not. In public he was apt to have a folded handkerchief in his hand, its purpose to wipe perspiration from his face. His habitual dress, like Zeke Vanderhooven's, was a white linen suit, a white shirt, a black string tie, and a broad-brimmed hat.

Another regular attendee was Jim-Joe Peterson, M.D., whose success as a physician was widely known and much respected. His reputation rested mainly on his ability to treat patients who were afflicted with pneumonia, a disease often called the "old folks relief" because it was so often fatal to elderly persons. It also accounted for the deaths of many young persons. Doctor Peterson would often go to the home of a pneumonia patient and, as he described it, "camp out" there. By being in constant attendance, he could administer whatever medication was needed. A caring man whose breezy manner belied his seriousness, Peterson often bemoaned the lack of any really effective drug against the malady.

In addition to his fame as a physician, he carried with him a secondary reputation—that of a drunkard, a term for which later generations would substitute "alcoholic." When he lost a patient, his anger—to him, his failure—could only be relieved by the release he found in alcohol. He was honest enough to admit this flaw, this demon which would eventually hasten his death. He was also honest enough to admit that his addiction could affect his judgment enough to be a danger to his patients. So when he became engulfed in alcohol, he would admit himself into a private sanitarium for treatment. At such times all of Midville would wait uneasily for his return—for in his absence the only local physician was Thomas Randolph Starkie, a self-important practitioner who also held the office of coroner.

A controversial member of the group was Edgar Allan Igo, the pastor of a locally organized congregation, the New World Church. He was a liberal's liberal in matters of religion. His tolerance of varying, even opposing, beliefs was well known and often condemned by more orthodox preachers in Midville. He was convinced that drinking alcohol in moderation was no sin; why else would Jesus have created gallons and gallons of wine at the Cana marriage feast? He had no objection to divorce if a couple was so incompatible that they were miserable and their children damaged by the conflict. He believed and taught that religious faith was very personal and it was the responsibility of the individual to determine his concept of God and his relationship with the deity. He taught that atonement and forgiveness were a function of the individual's relationship to God and could not be dictated by anyone else. He was convinced that women were oppressed and had been so since the days of Moses.

A reputation such as Igo's was an open target for fundamentalists who claimed to accept their interpretations of scripture as literal truth, the Word of God. Consequently, his congregants were targets also. The little church and its pastor furnished subject matter for frequent sermons as delivered by the Reverend Mike Wycliffe Amos, a hell-fire and damnation pastor of the most fundamental of the fundamentalist churches. Amos' sermons were delivered at a feverish pace and in the pitch of a scream. He taught that God was a God of anger; that He was crouching behind every corner and every bush, always ready to leap out and destroy the errant sinner.

Amos referred to the New World Church as "that bunch of ig-norant sinners that I urge you to include in your prayers" or "that den of iniquity that God has disowned." He saved his most vitupera-tive venom for Igo himself, often referring to him as "that ill-begotten son of Satan who has misled his congregation into certain perdition." Rev. Amos never translated his violent urges into per-sonal action, of course—he wasn't one to get his hands dirty! But there were in his congregation some who were not so restrained, and who rode at night with a band of "Whitecappers" whose brutal mission it was to pick up where the old-time Ku Klux Klan had left off.

Edgar Igo was aware of the criticism aimed at him. He could scarcely miss the reactions of some of Amos' flock whenever he chanced to meet them on the street—the women's averted eyes, the men's sullen stares. But if he was ever concerned with such behav-ior, he never showed it. If by chance he came into contact with the Rev. Mike, he greeted him warmly, much to the chagrin of the latter.

George Washington Mabry, affectionately known as "Wash," was the high sheriff of the county. In stature, he was not an impos-ing figure, standing five feet six inches in height, and slightly over-weight. His best physical asset was his ability (which many doubted until they saw it in action) to outrun any man who attempted to avoid arrest by fleeing. He seldom carried a weapon. Upon learning of a crime, he would often simply send word to any suspect to come voluntarily to the county jail for questioning. Such was his reputa-tion for getting his prisoner that he rarely had to go in search of a fugitive.

Wash Mabry knew the people of the county, not only those who could vote, but those whose lives had been depressed by chance or by conscious act. He was by nature a humanitarian—a weakness, arguably, considering that he dealt so often with criminals. But he loved people, all people, and never seemed to lose faith in people who wanted to turn their lives around. For families who, for whatever reason, were suffering and needy, he would visit community churches to organize food collection. Likewise he would collect money for medical treatment. Mabry and his beloved wife Parilee could not have children, a fact which seemed to produce in them a heartfelt affinity for all children. They often kept destitute children in their home until the parents could recover themselves. And if (as often happened) the parents were no longer on the scene, they placed the children in the homes of kind people—in effect, with foster parents approved by Sheriff and Mrs. Mabry.

A natural addition to the group was Miss Effie Alexander, the county librarian. She was a petite woman, with graying swept-back hair. She was a mere five feet tall. She habitually wore outdated high-button shoes, much-resoled. She was forced to exist on the pittance of a salary paid her by the county. But her love for books and a well-developed willingness to forgo luxuries allowed her a happy, if poverty-stricken existence.

She was a compulsive reader, having read every volume in the little library, as well as whatever printed matter she could glean through occasional visits to public libraries in Rome and Gadsden. Consequently, she had gained a very wide knowledge of authors and their products. She could quote from the works of William Shakespeare with the ease and confidence of a professor of English literature.

Miss Alexander had lobbied the county commission for years for authority to charge a two-cent rental for each book checked out by library patrons. The purpose of the fees was to provide funds for the purchase of books to replace those which were wear-worn or had missing pages. She eventually succeeded in not only getting the rental fee approved, but in getting the budget increased from ten to fifteen dollars a month. These actions gave such a boost to the size of the library that she had to collect nail kegs and scrap lumber to construct extra shelving to accommodate the new volumes. All this made Miss Effie very proud, so proud that she would often stand in the door and invite passersby to enter and inspect the new acquisitions. The library was her life, her obsession.

Miss Effie was also an amateur historian. Her interest as a historian did not exceed the boundaries of the county. She was not drawn to knowledge of who won which national election. She centered her efforts on the events and the people of Chufenee County. Being a librarian and a member of the Triple S Club, she was privy to much of the talk, the tragedies, the celebrations which occurred in the county. She remembered—sometimes only too well—what her patrons were reading, and what they said when they came to her seeking information. These conversations stood her in good stead as she worked on her great project—compiling a list of every local person who had served in the Confederate Army.

Miss Effie's list was subdivided into separate sections which contained names of those who had suffered fatal wounds, those who were wounded and had survived, and those who had lived through the entire conflict without significant wounds. The last list was by far the shortest of the three. During the current year she was putting together a list of those men who had died since April 1865. It would prove to be her longest list. Outside the library she had interviewed many of the county's Confederate veterans, though she had yet to interview J.P. Her efforts had often proven invaluable in proving veterans' claims when the state began paying a small monthly stipend to bona fide veterans of the Confederacy. A forceful personality if a bit of a gossip, she was a do-gooder with strict personal standards.

The club's only academic was Ezekiel Vanderhooven, headmaster of Chufenee Academy, which was located in the nearby hamlet of Gayleton. Much debate and discussion had occurred in recent decades concerning the establishment of a public high school—a hope resulting from measures proposed in the state legislature. As the years had passed and the proponents of state-supported high schools had gained support, county officials grudgingly considered how and when they would comply with state mandates. But the new century had seen no definitive action by either state or county, and Chufenee Academy remained the area's chief institution of secondary education.

By occupying the position of headmaster and with his reputation as a master of oratory, an art which was much admired by the public, Zeke was held in universal public esteem. That was a position he much enjoyed. That he was well-educated and intelligent was taken for granted .The fact that he was held in respect which bordered on awe—that was a holdover from the nineteenth century when any school teacher was an admired and respected person.

Zeke was the grandson of Dutch immigrants who had come to the United States, landing in Boston in 1830. His grandfather was a dairy herdsman who could find no employment with a dairy around Boston. He moved several times in search of a place to utilize his talents; and each move he made was in a southerly direction from Boston. He eventually found work on a large dairy farm in rural South Carolina, a position which would lead to a very close and profitable relationship between the emigrant Vanderhoovens and the owner of the farm.

It was on that farm that Zeke's father had grown up and under the grandfather's tutelage had become herdsman for a nearby farm. Ezekiel grew to young adulthood on that farm, and his father had expected him to also become a dairy herdsman. But at a young age, Ezekiel became fascinated with books, all sorts of books. His excellent recitations, along with his eclectic temperament, gained the attention of his teachers. One teacher in particular urged him to attend the nearby land grant college, writing such glowing recommendations that Ezekiel was granted a full four-year scholarship. This failed to impress his father until he agreed to study dairy science. But dairy science failed to quench young Zeke's appetite for a broader scope of knowledge, a fact which caused him to change his course of study to the general area of education concerned with teaching, a move which he carefully and with some difficulty kept secret from his father.

Eventually, Zeke revealed his secret to his parents, much to his father's disappointment and disgust. Such was the rift between him and his father that he returned home only briefly. Alone and without income, he became an itinerant tutor, teaching the children of affluent families in exchange for little more than room and board. Ever on the move, he accepted one job after another, seemingly always going farther south and west until he found himself in Chufenee County. After establishing a reputation as an effective teacher, he applied for and was accepted as headmaster of Chufenee Academy. There he was much admired and highly respected for his ability to teach—and to deliver speeches.

Supplier of refreshments for the club was Homer Henderson of the Sand Valley community, northwest of Midville. He was an unmarried man who, somewhat like J.P. and Cynthia, lived the life of a hermit. He was one of the more highly-regarded producers of corn whiskey in Chufenee County. Nobody knew his recipe for the beverage, but everybody knew it was scrupulously made to his own standards and was some of the safest and best moonshine available. Around strangers he was withdrawn, having little to say. With friends he was warm, talkative, and demonstrated a sense of humor. He came to meetings of the Triple S Club carrying his product in a half-gallon pharmaceutical flask.

Henderson's dress was severely informal, consisting of faded bib overalls, a blue work shirt, and a felt hat that had seen considerable service. If the temperature was below freezing he wore an old suit-coat; otherwise he wore no outer covering. He provided the whiskey without charge, always giving it to Miss Crissy for distribution, typically in the form of toddies.

The serving of alcohol at meetings of the Triple S Club consistently raised the hackles of the county's hell-fire-and-damnation preachers. The club's custom of loquacious libations was often good for a few Sunday sermons; occasionally a few righteous souls denounced the Triple S in letters to the *Midville Messenger*. Taking their cue from Reverend Igo, the Society members never discussed these rantings.

The final person attending meetings of the Triple S Club was Tolivar Hardcastle, owner, publisher, editor, and business manager of the weekly *Midville Messenger*. When asked how many employees the paper had, he would reply: "The paper has five employees and I am all of them." If he had an editorial policy, it was well-hidden. He was just as apt to criticize one political party as another, and he had gained a certain fame for his acerbic attacks on local politicians he deemed incompetent or corrupt. He had been sued several times for slander, libel, and defamation of character, but had always been able to prove his claims. Several politicians had either been denied election or had been removed from office as a result of his efforts. How and where he gained his information was seldom fully disclosed—often guessed at.

Hardcastle had never married, claiming that the paper was enough of a burden for any man. But he did have two great, consuming loves—dogs and whiskey. On the front page of each issue of the *Midville Messenger* was a recipe for a homemade cure for mange. The recipe always included a warning to protect the canine patient from getting wet.

As Sheriff Mabry once stated, Hardcastle had never been drunk, nor had he ever been quite sober. That he had a taste for fine whiskey was proven by the fact that, for years, he would drink no whiskey that was not produced by a duly licensed and bonded distillery. During this time he had ordered his drinking whiskey from a well-known supplier in Tennessee. That is, until he sampled Homer Henderson's product. He then pronounced that whiskey to be superior to any other.

The contents of the *Messenger* included mostly generic "boiler plate" from various syndication services. Unless there was a local event of significant news value, only the editorials and reports from community news correspondents had to be typeset. The paper did not own a linotype machine, so typesetting was done by hand. Depending on the degree of Hardcastle's intoxication, it was not unusual for entire lines of type to be inserted upside down and reversed. Hardcastle never offered an apology for the mechanical slips, if indeed he ever noticed them.

These were the faces and personalities J.P. Kinsor encountered at the home of Ambrose McKye and his widowed sister Christina McKye Dobbs. He was always greeted warmly, always accorded an immediate and nonjudgmental acceptance by the group. Not one person exhibited any pretension of superiority, nor was anyone made to feel inferior. If any gathering of people can be called democratic, this group was democratic. If anyone noticed J.P. Kinsor's disability, it was not mentioned. Wounded ex-soldiers were a common sight well into the twentieth century.

12

Questions and Answers

The subjects of conversation at meetings ranged from county gossip to the meaning of philosophical truths. Usually, J.P. sat silently and listened in amazement as the unmoderated discussion waxed and waned. As he witnessed the group's dynamics, he was impressed with how a group of people from such dissimilar backgrounds could absorb and respect opinions which were radically different from their own.

One evening late in July 1906, about a year after he attended his first meeting, the conversation started when Ambrose McKye asked Sheriff Wash Mabry if he had any new prisoners.

"Yes, I've arrested Ansel Deavors for beating his wife and child. He is now in jail, unable to make bond."

At this point, Dr. Jim-Joe Peterson joined in with the statement, "I treated both his wife and little boy for various bruises—a fractured arm for the boy and broken ribs for his wife. In addition she had lost a tooth." Then with a sad self-deprecatory shake of the head: "That man has been more or less drunk for years, and it's turned him into a monster."

"Sounds like a good project for the Whitecappers," said Edward Raye, referring to recent outbreaks of Klan-like violence in Alabama's hill country. "It is the sort of intervention clearly within their purview."

"That would only make matters worse," said Pastor Igo. "Masked intervention might cause any number of bad things to happen. The worst from a family viewpoint would be to cause Deavors to flee, leaving his wife and child without support. Or they could tie him to a tree and beat him so severely that he would be permanently disabled. Or they might kill him."

"Ed, I know you have very strong feelings concerning family violence," interjected Wash Mabry. "But in almost all cases I have experienced, violence begets more violence. These secret organizations make violence a way of life. It remains to be seen how their actions will play out in our society—you know I'm skeptical of anyone who has to hide behind a pillowcase! But surely you don't advocate the loss of a small boy's father. I have talked at length with Ansel Deavors. He is 'shamed; he bitterly regrets the injuries to his wife and son. He has promised—not for the first time, of course—that he will quit drinking and will do what he can to support his family. Years ago, he was a decent person. I pray that he can be a decent person again."

"Perhaps you and Pastor Igo can reform him," was Raye's sarcastic reply. Then, with an uneasy glace at Dr. Peterson: "Let us all hope for your success in weaning him away from the urges of a drunkard. This I know, if Deavors has a conscience and if he truly regrets his beastly behavior, he must carry the cognizance of his actions for the remainder of his life, and I guess that will be more punishing than any Whitecapping could be."

Tolivar Hardcastle joined the discussion by reciting Deavors' history of violence toward his family. "I counted three prior arrests of this monster, as reported in the *Messenger*. All three events occurred within the past three years. The record shows that in each case he promised to remain sober. And in each case he was given a nominal fine and set free. Apparently he has no intent to clean up his violent behavior. And from what I hear"—this with a quizzical glance in Mabry's direction—"he has ridden with the Whitecappers himself, sometimes."

"He has tried repeatedly to buy whiskey from me," said Homer Henderson. "I have always refused to sell to drunkards, and I certainly refuse to give out the fuel for wife-beatings. Maybe a few years in a chain gang would cure some of his drunken meanness."

Zeke Vanderhooven joined the conversation by observing: "This is a classic example of why I believe the lack of education is a major cause of such human behavior as you have all described. I am convinced that the more classical learning we experience, the more refined and gentle we become. I know that physical punishment of students does not improve their performance in school. Instead it hardens their resolve to defy authority and discipline! And I can think of no reason why the same result does not ensue from the physical punishment of adults."

Zeke gathered up the room with his eyes, and continued: "In working with my students, I try to find some example of good behavior and reward it with sincere praise. In many cases, I must expect only a glimpse of potential character, some small hint of goodness, or of ambition. I believe that there is some measure of goodness in the worst of us, and some evil in the best of us. That is to say that none of us is perfect, and none of us is entirely evil. In the case of Deavors, we must look past the fact that he drinks to excess. We must seek to learn why he drinks. There must be some demon in his life that tortures him until he drowns his soul in alcohol. But alcohol does not erase one's troubles; it only irrigates and aggravates them."

At this point, Ambrose McKye rejoined the discussion. "As a trial lawyer, I can see that if you all were a jury panel sitting in judgment of Ansel Deavors, the case would end as a mistrial. As individuals, you have expressed valid and honest opinions, but I can't see you, as a group, arriving at a common verdict."

Edward Raye asked: "Who needs the findings of a petit jury anyway? Leave legal discussions to a judge who has a law degree, who has trial experience as a practicing lawyer, and who can analyze evidence without the bias of provincial attitudes. A few years ago I served on a jury hearing a suit for damages. As we entered the jury room, one member of the panel sat in a chair, leaned back against the wall and said, 'Wake me when you arrive at five thousand dollars.' Is that justice? Laymen tend to have vast misconceptions about law; and often they have a warped, or rather, flawed view of what is just."

Again Zeke drew himself up, and commented: "The jury system of administering justice has a long history. Socrates in ancient Greece faced a jury of five hundred of his Athenian peers. The undergirding philosophy of a jury is that all respectable men know right from wrong, and when faced with the obligation to judge, they inherently strive to make just decisions. That is why convicted felons lose citizenship, including the right to vote and the privilege of jury service. Edward, I'm sure you and the other members of that jury proceeded to a just verdict in spite of one radical member. The jury system is not perfect; mistakes are made; but there are ways to correct and atone for any miscarriage of justice."

Edward Raye replied: "Yes, that was a very astute and effective panel of jurors. After the trial we reported that juror's behavior to the presiding judge. The judge removed his name from the county jury pool. He will never serve on another jury."

This dialog was interrupted by Miss Crissy's announcement that the meal was ready. Delnora, the long-time family cook, had prepared the food as only she was capable, and had displayed it cafeteria-style on the dining room table. Members of the Sagacious Sophomore Society arose as one to form a line at the table. To eat a meal prepared by Delnora was an adventure to cherish. They piled food on the plates as if they were day laborers who had been denied their noon meal. As they regained their seats, food and drink in hand, the conversation resumed but was subdued in volume and pitch. Several members complimented Delnora's cooking, to which she modestly replied "Thank y'all."

Miss Effie Alexander had remained silent during the previous discussion and throughout the dinner. As noted previously, her life was wrapped up in the county library; she was always planning for improvements in physical equipment or for ways to better serve the public. She was now about to undertake her most ambitious project ever: the addition of a legal library where not only could lawyers research questions of law, but common citizens could have access to the Alabama and United States codes. She now spoke up.

"I get newsletters from librarians in adjoining counties, some of whom have recently purchased books of law. They submit glowing reports of how well those acquisitions have been received and used. The Chufenee County Library has never owned even so much as a legal periodical, and I am ashamed of that! I am about to ask the Board of County Commissioners to allocate a modest amount of money on an annual basis to begin the purchase of copies of the state code. Unless they are prodded to approve that request by people such as you folks, they are apt to ignore it. So I am asking you to lend your influence to get the request approved, and also to ask your friends for their support."

"Let me comment on that," stated Ambrose McKye. "While I have a complete legal library in my office, I can see why Miss Effie's request has much merit. My library has been accumulating since my grandfather began his practice. My father and I have continued to subscribe to annual editions of the state code and the *Alabama Reports*. A library such as mine is very expensive if purchased as a whole and, in fact, is beyond the financial reach of a beginning attorney. I can't estimate how much usage would occur by the general public; however, it would be an extremely valuable addition to our library. So I join Miss Effie in urging you to help convince the county commission to set aside whatever money she has requested."

At this point Wash Mabry's deputy Fred Bankston had been admitted to the home by Delnora. He motioned to Mabry to join him in the kitchen. Mabry followed him from the dining room where the deputy announced in a low voice, "this afternoon Alfred Ensor was found dead, in the bushes near his buggy, down the road from Eau Claire Springs."

The sheriff returned to the meeting and said, "I must leave now to investigate a matter which has come up. Thank you, Miss Crissy and Delnora, for another great meal."

The remaining members sat in silence for a short time, and it was apparent that the deputy's attempt at discretion had been in vain. Then Edward Raye asked: "How old was Mr. Ensor?"

"He must have been in his seventies," answered Jim-Joe Peterson. "His health's been fragile for years—I treated him for a slight case of pneumonia last winter—and he was perhaps inclined to drink too much. Sheriff Mabry probably won't do much about it until my colleague, Coroner Starkie, assembles a coroner's jury to investigate the circumstances of this death."

"Don't worry—I'll print in next week's paper whatever report may be made," said Tolivar Hardcastle. "Did you know him, J.P.?" he asked. "He was found not far from your place."

J.P. admitted that he had known Ensor slightly, enough to sell him the occasional bottle of whiskey. He said nothing more, since it was his practice to say little of his own or his wife's modest business dealings.

"Mr. Ensor's death is a reminder that life is so uncertain," added Miss Alexander, breaking what might have been an awkward silence.

Edward Raye turned the discussion to a deeper level by saying: "We don't even know what life is. The book of Genesis states that God breathes life into a newborn child. The same book of the Old Testament states that God is a spirit, and if that be true, life is spiritual in nature. The scientist will say that life is the sum of all bodily functions, and he may go so far as to state that the spirit or soul does not exist. Or if it does exist, it is not relevant to active existence."

"A great philosopher has stated that he will not include among his friends anybody who knowingly steps on a worm," piped up Miss Alexander. "That is a good example of how we should respect the force we call life. We do know that what we call life exists at the expense of other life. To preserve our sense of delicacy, we call it the food chain. In order for one life form to continue, other life forms are consumed."

Dr. Jim-Joe interrupted at this point to say, "I have witnessed the birth of many children. I have witnessed the death of many people, too. I must admit that I do not know what the life force is, but whatever it is, I have a profound respect for it, and I share the feeling expressed in Miss Effie's quote from the unknown philosopher."

Edgar Igo had remained silent during this phase of discussion. Now he said: "Let us consider for a moment what we all can relate to! I'm sure we can all agree that nothing just happens—it is caused to happen. Every event in the history of the universe had a causal force. We can trace causes and their results all the way back to the first cause. This is where theologians and scientists often differ. We can safely assume that the universe did not just happen—it had a cause. The question then is what or who caused that singular event? The first verse of the first chapter of St. John's writings states: 'In the beginning was the Word, and the Word was of God, and the Word was God.' Notice that 'Word' was capitalized, and if we trace the etymology of 'Word,' we finally arrive at the Greek *logos*, which in translation means intelligence. That is a much cleaner and clearer description than that of the book of Genesis, which states that God created the earth and all that is in it, on it, or above it. Genesis gives only a vague glimpse of the nature of God. No great leap of faith is needed to believe that some form of intelligence was required to create the universe. And, yes, there is much chaos in the universe, but there is much more order."

Pastor Igo then continued, "a French philosopher, whose name I have forgotten, once calculated the chances of a spontaneous or random creation. Using arithmetical notation he came to the conclusion that there was one chance in 1×10^{78} power of a causeless creation. That is 10 followed by 78 zeroes. We don't have a name for that number, it is so large. It is like so many of our concepts of limitations—or alternately for the lack of limits. We have invented words for what we can't grasp mentally or physically. Eternity, endless, infinity, continuous, forever, and the list can go on and on. Logic will tell us that these words are impossibilities, unless time is circular. Or perhaps time travels along a straight line, turns around and repeats its path in reverse. Can it be that time will eventually wash up on the shore of eternity, reverse directions in a chronological rip-tide and return in the direction from which it came? Or is time circular in nature, always traveling in one direction? Of course, we don't know the answers and probably will never know."

After a brief hesitation he continued, anticipating a great thinker of the twentieth century: "'God may be subtle, but he is not cruel.' He created man and the universe, but he left an unimaginable number of unknowns. Man has busied himself with solving these unknowns; potentially there is vast harvest of mysteries that he can gather for eons to come."

Ambrose McKye joined the discussion by observing: "Many people have talked themselves into trouble by challenging the status quo. As examples I can name Socrates, Galileo, and Jesus. Socrates challenged the existing hierarchy of gods as worshipped by his fellow Greeks. Of course"—and here he dropped into the sarcastic tone so effective in the courtroom—"he was charged with corrupting the youth of Athens, convicted by a jury of five hundred, and executed by a forced diet of hemlock. Galileo was foolish enough to have novel thoughts about the planetary system, ending up in the pokey. Jesus violated the Mosaic Law, only to win a trip to Golgotha and on into history. All three were guilty of affronting entrenched religious rulers who were jealous of their power. In fact, we would be astounded if we could know the total of humans who have died as the result of religious tensions. Men of faith? Men of blood!"

There were others who had opinions to add, but librarian Alexander announced that she had to leave. The others followed, each thanking Miss Crissy and Delnora for the wonderful dinner. J.P. went on his way among them, thinking to himself that Cynthia had lost a customer in old man Ensor.

While he was thinking, J.P. was on his way to unhitch Dixie, an even-tempered bay horse he had acquired for next to nothing from a family that was, in the then-current phrase, "selling out and going to Texas." His thoughts were momentarily interrupted by a colorful flyer tacked to a fencepost. In lurid "chromo" colors it offered the services of "Nathaniel Courtney, Star Barber, Professor of the Tonsorial Art, and general Inspector of Craniums, who offers his services to the public with full confidence that in the Razor, Soap, and Perfume line his facilities are equal to the best." A handwritten note at the bottom invited customers to "Inquire at Jordan's Store." J.P. began to consider whether this self-inflating barber could somehow be a Courtney of Virginia. But these thoughts fled in turn as he undertook, painfully, to mount Dixie. After one embarrassing failure he accepted a hand-up from Edward Raye. Then he rode back to the Springs.

On his next trip into town however, he noticed that the placards were down. When he inquired of young Jeff Jordan, he was told that the barber, a well-preserved black man "not from hereabouts," had arranged to set up at the back of the store at irregular intervals. "Those posters of his are right foolish," Jeff continued, "but he does fine work and he *will* bring in the customers, especially once the crops are in." Looking at J.P.'s home-trimmed locks, he added: "Maybe you'll be trying him yourself?"

"I very well might," responded J.P., his thoughts elsewhere.

13

Inconclusive Conclusions

Citizens of Midville and Chufenee County were abuzz with speculation concerning the death of Alfred Ensor. He was a semi-wealthy farmer. His reputation was that of a solid citizen who was family-oriented, who was active in his church, and who in fact had donated five acres of valuable bottom land, upon which the church was built. Members of the congregation had expressed their appreciation and respect by naming the church Ensor's Chapel and by electing him chairman of the board of trustees of the church.

Sheriff Mabry soon received the coroner's jury report on the intriguing circumstances of Ensor's demise. The report only added to speculation with the predictable statement that "Alfred Ensor was found near Eau Claire Springs, dead from cause or causes undetermined." The testimony they heard had shown there was no evidence of foul play; but there was evidence of a painful death as indicated by the fetal position of the body and disturbed soil surrounding the body. An empty bottle had been found by the body and a distinct odor of alcohol emitted from the corpse. The apparently sudden death of Mr. Ensor might have been caused by the ingestion of a violent poison, or conceivably by natural causes—if Demon Rum could be classed as such an agent—but the citizens were unable to determine either a toxin or a definitive bodily breakdown.

On a Wednesday shortly following Ensor's passing, Tolivar Hardcastle published his obituary in the *Midville Messenger*.

> Yesterday, the deceased body of Mr. Alfred Ensor was found at the edge of Eau Claire Springs. Doctor T.R. Starkie impaneled a coroner's jury, the report from which stated that they were unable to determine a cause of death.
>
> Funeral services were held Monday past at Ensor's Chapel Church with burial in the adjoining cemetery. Mr. Ensor is survived by his widow, Adelina, and by a son, John Roy. A charitable man, he leaves behind a good reputation, a loving family, and grateful neighbors, which is as much as anybody among us can hope for upon departing this vale of tears.

The next morning, Ambrose McKye and Dr. Jim-Joe Peterson were enjoying their usual cups of coffee at the Elite Café when Reverend Igo entered and joined them. He had a copy of the *Midville Messenger* and pointed to Ensor's obituary.

"Brother Tolivar finally found a bit of fresh news to print," remarked Igo. "That obituary is discreet. But the gossip now making the rounds ought to give Reverend Amos material for several of his hell-fire and damnation tirades. At least it may get him off my back for a while."

Dr. Peterson had read the obituary very thoroughly, twice. "That man was murdered," he said. "My guess is that someone gave him a strong dose of some cyanide compound. Cyanide has a distinct odor, which would be overcome by the stronger odor of whiskey. That could explain in part why the jury was unable to determine if he was poisoned, and if he was poisoned, what caused his death. Other poisons including arsenic would have affected him the same way, but arsenic would take longer to kill. Cyanide is very rapid in its actions on the body's functions, and it is also very painful. That might explain the apparent convulsions the deceased experienced in the throes of death."

"Why don't you run against Doc Starkie in the next Democratic primary?" asked Reverend Igo. "The county could use a man of your expertise."

"I don't have the time," said Dr. Jim-Joe. "And the pay is so low as to make it unattractive. Besides, it's not just the pay; it's the requirement for so many reports which must be sent to the State Department of Health. It appears that every clerk in the state capital must get a copy." Then, after a pause: "If T.R. lost out as coroner, he might leave town; and the community needs somebody to fill in when I'm—indisposed."

"From a legal point of view, a coroner's jury leaves much to be desired," said McKye, preventing an awkward moment. "Lay persons have no medical knowledge upon which to base a decision, but unfortunately a coroner's jury decision stands as a legal document. A coroner's jury cannot perform autopsies, nor can they perform chemical tests—and Starkie usually can't be bothered to carry out either of those. Thus, most jury decisions contain the words, 'from cause or causes undetermined.' I often wonder how many victims of undetected murder we bury each year."

From Dr. Peterson: "In med school and during my internship, I watched people die in intense pain from various poisons. That's not a pretty sight. I often hoped they'd die quickly. Many would die anyway, even after having their stomach pumped."

The three men then went their separate ways. And in a few days, the people of Midville became less curious about Ensor's death and returned to their workaday conversations. Of course the Reverend Amos found fuel for several sermons about the evils of whiskey and of those who drank it. A chorus of Amens arose from the Amen Corner each time he condemned the existence and use of alcohol. One of his most enthusiastic endorsers was none other than Ansel Deavors, whose sentence had been suspended after he promised Circuit Judge Holdbrook that he would, in the future, travel the teetotal road. In addition the Rev. Mike found it convenient to include Edgar Igo in his tirades, because: "I'm told they use *real wine* in the Communion ritual." On cue, members of the congregation exchanged scandalized looks; Deavors raised his Bible to hide a smile.

14

Position, Position

"A dollar a day beats the hell out of working your ass off trying to make a living farming!" was the emphatic opinion stated by Tanglefoot Jones to Frank Franklin. They were both employed by the Nelson Lumber Company sawmill; both lived in shacks located on a knoll a few hundred yards from the sawmill. Both were physically handicapped: Jones at birth with severely clubbed feet, and Franklin from a fall when a scaffolding collapsed while he was laying brick on a smokestack. The fall had resulted in numerous broken bones and the loss of his left arm near the shoulder. In spite of their handicaps, they were valued workers, each receiving five dollars each Friday at quitting time after working twelve hours per day for five days.

Saturdays were nonwork days, devoted by Jones and Franklin to drunkenness. They were friends, but not drinking buddies. They each preferred to drink alone, drinking until the alcohol overcame whatever pains their bodies contained and whatever worries inhabited their brains. Their alcoholic euphoria lasted from Friday night until Sunday noon when their whiskey was gone and their befogged brains began to emerge from la-la land.

For several years, now, their source for whiskey had been Cynthia Kinsor. Her product, as already noted, was potent but safe. For years, local folk and a number of passersby had sought out her whiskey. She said little during these transactions, while J.P. sat mute in the background—or on good days helped her to fill the jars. For their part, regular clients like Tanglefoot and Frank had little to say; others were strangers, men who happened to be in the neighborhood. Some of the latter talked openly to each other, speaking out unguardedly in the belief that Cynthia was simple-minded.

Each Friday in the late afternoon, Jones and Franklin would appear at the Kinsor home to purchase their weekend supply of whiskey. Both came with a quart size Mason jar. They paid their dollar and a quarter, took their whiskey and went their separate ways.

Neither man was married; neither had family responsibilities. Their consumption of alcohol was harmful to no one except themselves. Franklin preferred to return to his sawmill shack, go to bed and drink himself into an alcoholic euphoria. He ate nothing from Friday noon until Sunday noon; the only nutrition his body received was the empty calories of the alcohol. The wonder was that, in spite of the physical trauma he had suffered from the fall from the scaffolding, his body was able to metabolize the alcohol. He was always able to return to work on Monday morning. His job as a lumber offbearer was one which had exhausted a series of predecessors, causing them to quit. Franklin had learned to use the stub of his severed arm as a counterpoise in lifting and carrying the resin-laden pine boards. The distance from the point of pick-up to the edger was some ten yards, where he would deposit the bark-edged boards to be dimensioned to a nominal width, clear of any bark. His ability to do this work caused the sawmill owner to overlook his drinking habit, as he considered him a valued worker.

Tanglefoot Jones, on the other hand, would usually wander away as far as the Springs, where he would swallow ample gulps of neat moonshine, chased by spring water. As the alcohol took effect, easing his body pain and tension, he would sing snatches of the hymn *Nearer My God to Thee*, or alternately *God Be with You 'Til We Meet Again*. As the anesthetic effect of the alcohol deepened, he would sink into a stupor, lying very still and peaceful. Then as the alcoholic nirvana wore off, he would drink more whiskey and return to a state of blissful quiet.

His favorite place at the Springs was an area where a mixture of fallen leaves and reed grass formed a soft mat upon which he lay. The area was located behind a cluster of willow sprouts and a few feet from the edge of the lagoon. Here he was relatively invisible to passers-by, but close enough to the water's edge to easily get water for cooling his throat after swallowing the raw liquor.

In mild weather, Jones was perfectly safe. But in winter he faced the danger of sudden drops in the temperature which, coupled with the depressive effect of whiskey, could be fatal. In fact, he had once been found by Ed Raye almost frozen, face down at the water's edge, his breathing shallow and very slow. Raye had half-carried, half-dragged Jones to his nearby house where he was wrapped in quilts and given warm water to drink. His recovery was slow but steady. By Sunday noon he was able to walk and insisted on returning to his sawmill shack. By Monday morning he was at his accustomed job, although his movements were labored and painful.

This practice of drinking themselves into an alcoholic stupor became a ritual for Franklin and Jones. Jones' alcoholic escapades at the Springs meant that he would be in an ideal position—if not an ideal condition—to see whatever might go on there.

15

Second Strike

As is true of most small towns, after only a few days the speculation and rumor surrounding the death of Alfred Ensor subsided. The populace of Chufenee County was almost entirely an agrarian one, made up of subsistence farmers, farmers who derived their food and fiber from the land. Such existence demanded close attention and long hours of hard labor. The super-critical preachers of the area resumed their attacks on card playing, dancing, and demon alcohol. Some even found the use of hairpins by women to be a cardinal sin. And woe be unto a woman who cut her hair short! She was little more than a harlot and was hopelessly on the road to hell.

It had been many years since Federal troops had patrolled the small towns of the Confederacy. Scalawags and Carpetbaggers had long since been neutralized or driven out. Hill country leaders had emerged—emerged triumphant, benefitting from an alliance with Blackbelt planters, who for their part were determined to subdue former slaves to a permanent state of dependence. A landlord-sharecropper society had resulted from the redistribution of labor all over the state. Yet if you paid attention to political oratory, the sectional hatred associated with Civil War and Reconstruction had subsided but little. Some of J.P. Kinsor's contemporaries remained as rebellious as ever, willing upon any occasion to call forth their wartime emotions. J.P. usually contented himself with saying: "We surrendered, but we wasn't whipped." Sometimes he would add: "We was unvanquished."

One fine Saturday early in March 1907, Jones and Franklin appeared at the Kinsor house for their weekly supply of whiskey; J.P. took their money and handed the quart bottles to them. As usual, Franklin returned to his sawmill shack, while Jones stopped at the springs. He drank deeply of the corn whiskey, sighed deeply, sat down and closed his eyes. After a time he scrambled to his feet and moved toward his accustomed place behind the low-growing bush. To his disappointment, he found it already occupied by a man who appeared to be asleep, his horse nearby.

As Jones approached the motionless body, a leg twitched, the eyelids fluttered, and then the entire body tensed and quivered in one great convulsion. Then the body was very still. Jones was puzzled and annoyed—puzzled at the odd movements and annoyed that the stranger was usurping his favorite place at the Springs. And what was that in the corner of his eye? What rustling? Was it his Ma? He sometimes saw her, he'd swear, when he'd had just enough to drink. Sometimes she just looked down on him. Sometimes she'd help him sing the hymns. He turned back to the interloper.

"Hey Bo'! Wake up," Jones ordered.

There was no reaction from the now still body.

"Man, you've got my place. Wake up and go somewhere else," he said as his impatience increased.

Then Jones looked at the half-open, unseeing eyes of the man and realized that he had died. He immediately made his labored way up the hillside to the home of Edward Raye. Raye was as usual sitting on his front porch.

Tanglefoot Jones was short of breath as a result of his climbing the steep hill, combined with the excitement of seeing a man die before his very eyes.

"Mr. Ed, they's a dead man down there at the Springs," was all the information he could give.

"Who is he?" asked Raye.

"I don't know, I never saw him before," replied Jones. "He's got a fine saddle horse waiting under that big oak tree."

Then both men walked back to the Springs. Raye immediately recognized the corpse. He observed that the leaves and grass around the body were flattened and scattered, obviously a result of painful convulsions and thrashing of the arms and legs of the deceased. A mostly empty pint jar of whiskey was lying near the body.

"Who's he?" asked Jones.

"He's Mr. Delroy Dobbs. He owns a large farm out in the Lindale community," answered Raye. "He's a supply merchant and he sometimes comes out this way on business."

"I wonder why he stopped at the Springs, and I also wonder how come he died," pondered Jones.

Ignoring Jones' curiosity, Raye said: "We must notify the sheriff. He will want to know, and probably will ask Doc Starkie to assemble a coroner's jury. The great processes of the Common Law, centuries-old, must be applied to the situation at hand." Then, noticing that Jones wasn't listening, he spoke more to the point: "I'll watch the body; you go get the sheriff. Go to my barn and bridle one of my mules and ride into Midville." Seeing Jones' hesitation, he added: "I'll have something for you to drink—a fair-sized libation—when you get back."

Jones went to Raye's barn, selected a mule, bridled it, and led it to a tree stump along the barnyard fence. He mounted the stump, from which he was able to get astride the mule. As he departed for Midville, toes turned inward and touching the mule's sides, Jones was a comical figure.

"They's a dead man at the Springs," blurted out Jones as he arrived at Wash Mabry's office.

"Who is he?" inquired the sheriff.

"I don't rec'lect—Ed Raye knowed him—but he's dead sho' 'nuf."

"Dead man at the Springs is becoming a habit," observed Mabry. "Go on back to the Springs and tell Edward Raye to get six men together where the body is located, and tell them I'll be there with Doctor Starkie as soon as we can get there. And warn them not to disturb the body or the area surrounding it."

Immediately after Jones left his office, the sheriff sent a deputy to Starkie's surgery, then busied himself with gathering state-required forms to be executed by a coroner's jury. As he entered the hallway, he met Tolivar Hardcastle who asked where he was going. He gave Hardcastle the news of the latest death at the Springs. The newspaperman then stated that he would attend the coroner's jury proceedings himself. The two men saddled their horses and made their way to the death scene.

Mabry and Hardcastle arrived at the Springs within three-quarters of an hour. They didn't have to wait much more than an hour before they were joined by the diminutive Dr. Starkie, unprepossessing in his too-big black coat, clearly fussed at the prospect of yet another suspicious death. While each man scribbled notes after a brief examination of the body and its surroundings—autopsies, as mentioned, not being Starkie's style—Ed Raye came up with five of his neighbors. As soon as they arrived, Starkie set about organizing the half-dozen men into a jury, appointing Raye as foreman. Next Mabry handed Starkie the packet of forms required by the state; Starkie passed them on to Ray.

Mabry declared that the corpse was that of one Delroy Dobbs. From the condition of the grass and the soil under and around the body, it was obvious that Dobbs had died in anguish. The convulsions of his body and limbs had flattened the grass and disturbed the soil around his body.

Edward Ray assembled the jury. Reading from the top sheet of his packet of forms, he administered the oath of office and gathered them around the dead body. "We are charged with the solemn duty of determining as best we can the cause of Mr. Dobbs' demise," he said, importantly. "I am here reminded of a question raised by William Shakespeare in one of his plays: 'Who knows what evil lurks in the hearts of men?' We are here faced with the problem of determining who caused this man to die and, if possible, to learn what caused his death. I ask you men to observe carefully all visible aspects of the death scene and to report our findings to the sheriff for his use in locating and arresting the person or persons responsible."

Each juror viewed the body and the area surrounding it, noting the disturbed state of the soil and the flattened weed growth. They agreed that the tethered horse belonged to Mr. Dobbs and that the jar had contained white whiskey. They also noted that the odor of whiskey pervaded the area around the body. So, the conclusion was that the bottle belonged to Mr. Dobbs and that he had consumed the missing half-bottle. They agreed that when all these observations were considered as a whole, Mr. Dobbs died as a result of consuming whiskey which contained a toxic substance, the identity of which could not be determined.

As fairly often happened, the findings of the jury were not really findings of fact, but a summary of the obvious. The final sentence of the written report simply urged the sheriff to investigate all known sources of home-made whiskey.

Once again when news of Dobb's death reached the populace, the rumor mill resumed its inevitable production of half-truths and innuendo. Rumors ranged from suicide to murder, from being poisoned to falling off his horse, from drinking too much whiskey too fast to suffering heart failure. One report suggested that he was having a clandestine affair, was discovered by his paramour's husband and dispatched into eternity by the husband's revenge.

Rampant rumor can eventually approach truth, and so it was in the death of Delroy Dobbs. A majority of the population came to believe that his death was an act of revenge for his part in some prior action.

16
Musings

Sheriff Mabry pondered the facts as he knew them concerning the death of Delroy Dobbs. This was the second episode of mysterious death at the Springs, with both victims in possession of moonshine whiskey—whiskey most likely produced, as he came to believe, by Cynthia Kinsor. Both victims had consumed a portion of a jar of whiskey. Both had suffered a convulsive death. They were approximately the same age.

There was no direct evidence that Mrs. Kinsor was involved. All evidence was circumstantial and could not justify an arrest, scarcely even a formal interrogation. But she was and always had been an enigma. If she knew who she was prior to her husband's discovery of her badly beaten body, she had never revealed that information. Her life with J.P. had been that of a recluse, living quietly and seldom appearing outside the homestead. She had the reputation of being fiercely loyal and supportive of J.P. and their son March.

Months passed with no further evidence being made known. Delroy Dobbs was buried, his death relegated to the past as the populace pursued their chosen ways of life. Seemingly everyone except Wash Mabry was content to let the affair remain an unsolved mystery. Mabry may have been an unpretentious man, but he was persistent. The oath he swore when he assumed his office was a serious one. Consequently, he vowed to himself that he would exhaust every shred of evidence in order to bring justice in the case.

On a Monday morning as the regular crowd had gathered at the Elite for coffee and gossip, Sheriff Mabry and Dr. Jim-Joe Peterson were seated at their usual table. Their conversation was customarily light-hearted. Yet after a few minutes, Mabry began questioning the doctor about the reactions of the human body to various poisons.

"There are a number of chemicals which produce convulsions when ingested," said the physician. "Arsenic is one; strychnine is one; cyanide is another. I've been thinking about poisons, and I doubt that arsenic is what killed those two men. It is easily extracted from flypaper, but that is sold mostly in big cities. As for cyanide, it is not readily available; few people are even aware of its existence."

Then Mabry asked the doctor how any local person—for instance, a moonshiner—could obtain one of those poisons.

"Strychnine is a common rat poison. It is readily available at most stores in this area, and I think it will be found in most homes," replied the doctor.

"I feel that Mrs. Kinsor made the moonshine in each instance. Consider where the bodies were found! She may be involved in these crimes, but I can't proceed to make a case against her. I don't know her motive, if any, and I can't arrest her on the basis of my suspicion," said Sheriff Mabry.

The conversation continued for several minutes, finally drifting back to friendly banter and coffeehouse humor. As the courthouse clock tolled the hour of eight, the group broke up, each to his daily work. Mabry walked diagonally across Main Street to the court-house and to his office. The sheriff thought over his acquaintance with J.P. and his wife, reflecting for the thousandth time on how little we can know of even our friends. What evil, indeed, lurks in the hearts of men—or women?

He turned and followed Peterson toward his surgery, a small frame structure attached to his pleasant board-and-batten house. Just as the doctor was climbing the steps, Mabry called out to him, and catching up to him, added in a quieter tone: "I'd appreciate it, Jim-Joe, if you kept our conversation—both the what and the who—just between us."

17
Many a Slip

All over the country, the times were good. In particular, crop prices were well above the rock-bottom levels of the depression-ridden 1890s. Theodore Roosevelt was mid-way through his second term, and—even if they disliked him as a New York Republican—Alabamians respected the man's Cuban war record and responded to his general exuberance. Alabama's rabble-rouser B. B. Comer had been governor for nearly a year, and was now in the midst of a holy crusade to lower railroad rates; this, though he did not say so, was chiefly for the benefit of cotton mill owners like himself.

Chufenee County was not much affected by such disturbances. In fact it responded slowly to the increased modernization of the nation at large—though the lumbering automobiles of the time were occasionally seen on Midville's unpaved streets. True, telephones had become something of a commonplace in town and in the homes of prosperous farmers. Such citizens were beginning to subscribe to daily newspapers, some of which carried detailed business reports. Thus for the first time ever, a number of local men began to travel into the nearby city of Gadsden to arrange speculations on stock futures—or to communicate with their brokers via the new telegraph office in Midville. These latter developments had their positive and negative aspects—but whether the deals in question paid off or crashed, they generally meant more business for the better-regarded class of moonshiners, and Cynthia's small distillery was working overtime.

On a bright blue afternoon October 1907, an elderly man pulled his buggy to a stop in front of the Kinsor place, on his way to Midville from his home in the Sand Valley community a dozen miles away. He looked around slowly and with evident distaste, and might have driven on; but J.P. Kinsor, who was sitting on his front porch, hailed him.

"Want something, stranger?" said J.P.

"I've heard that a man might buy himself some corn whiskey here, Mr. Kinsor," said Lemuel Emerson, after a pause. "If so, I need it—need somethin' to brace myself. I wouldn't normally, but I think I may've had some bad luck."

Kinsor didn't follow the news reports—in fact he avoided them—but he knew that folks were nervous about the markets. He felt sorry for this old man, whom he vaguely remembered having seen at meetings of the Confederate veterans. He called out: "Cynthia? You've got a customer!" Slowly, from the back of the house, Emerson was aware that a bonneted figure had come onto the porch. The woman appeared to be speaking to Kinsor, who nodded, and said: "Cynthia doesn't like to sell to folks she don't know. You're not going to buy enough of her whiskey to sell, are you?"

"Unless I'm mistaken I won't have enough money left to set up in business," said Emerson, with a subdued attempt at humor. "Just bring me some of your stuff and let me pay for it. I need to quieten down my nerves."

The woman went back into the house, returning after a short time. The autumn sun beat down upon Mr. Emerson, who had climbed down from the buggy and stood fidgeting at the gate. The old couple walked slowly down the walkway, looking for all the world like Baucus and Philemon. Cynthia handed Emerson the bottle; Emerson passed a handful of silver over to J.P., observing: "Thank you kindly—I need something good!"

He faced them as he spoke, and for a moment, seemed struck by something about the woman. He looked at her for a long moment, then dropped his eyes. A moment more, and Cynthia said in a hoarse whisper: "Wait a bit longer, Mister—I know just what you need." J.P. looked questioningly at her, but she had already taken the pint jar out of Emerson's hands and turned back toward the house. In a short time she returned, a similar jar in her hands. She passed it to him over the gate, whispering: "This'll do you right. It's from my special batch."

When Emerson had driven off, J.P. protested: "You've not got no special batch, have you?"

She responded: "He needed something good, all right."

"You're a mite quare today, Cynthia," was his rejoinder. Then: "I think I'll have myself a nap before supper." Cynthia waited until he had had a chance to settle down, then slipped out of the gate and headed down toward the Springs.

18

Ruminations

It was one of those days of weak sun that comes in late November to Chufenee County. In fact it was Thanksgiving Day, and Wash Mabry was sitting in the front porch swing of his house, smoking a pipe and digesting a dinner that, in his opinion, couldn't be beat. He thought it was a pity that he and his wife (his lovely Parilee!) could not have had several children to help them enjoy such a feast. Certainly he had every reason to think that the four children who had shared with them the turkey, corn bread dressing, sweet potato soufflé, green peas, congealed salad, dinner rolls, and pumpkin pie—and who were cheerfully helping Parilee with the washing up, having been promised second servings of the pie—had enjoyed themselves thoroughly.

It was with similarly mixed thoughts that Wash Mabry mulled over the legal events of the past several weeks. How ole Lem' Emerson had driven, looking more dead than alive, into Midville, where he had been tended by Jim-Joe Peterson. How Jim-Joe had phoned up the sheriff's office as soon as he was certain that the old man was in stable condition. How he, Mabry, had been quick to interview the victim at the first opportunity. Which turned out to be the next morning, October eighteenth.

The sheriff recalled how Emerson had admitted to collapsing at the Springs, though he had seemed strangely reluctant to talk about it, had even made light of it. He was agitated, no doubt due to the ordeal he had undergone. Mabry was nothing if not patient, however. Assuming a casual tone, he had coaxed the full story out, letting Emerson think that he, Mabry, already knew all about it anyway. When Emerson spoke the words that positively placed Cynthia Kinsor at the scene, the sheriff had let out a sigh.

He had long sympathized with Cynthia Kinsor, whose physical deformities had kept her apart, a self-exile, from the people of town and countryside. Many of them, Mabry had sometimes thought, would have taken pleasure in befriending her—though in this regard, it may be that his thoughts were more a reflection of his own disposition than they were of Chufenee County attitudes. But even as he had thought kindly of Mrs. Kinsor, he had been aware of the chill that hung about her; and he had been quick to think that she had somehow been involved in the two peculiar deaths at the Springs.

"A coincidence," Mabry said often to himself and almost as often to his deputies, "is a gift horse that simply begs you to look in its mouth." He had said as much after Emerson's poisoning, when Emerson and Dr. Peterson had testified before a grand jury hastily convened on the initiative of District Attorney Urban Kirksey, an always-eager graduate of Professor Zeke's academy. The foreman had delivered the jurors' findings, a "true bill" accusing Cynthia Kinsor of trying to murder Emerson and of having murdered Ensor and Dobbs.

"Wha'd you see in that horse's mouth?" Jim-Joe had asked

Mabry, as he and several others met up afterwards in the sheriff's office.

"Not much," Wash had replied. "Not even a can of Rough-on-Rats was on the premises when I searched. I suspect that Cynthia has her ways of knowing things. One of her loyal customers, some courthouse loafer, may have tipped her off—told her I was getting a warrant. Lord knows that nothing around here is secret for long! If somebody passed her the warning, she had plenty of time to dump the poison somewhere and wash all the jars clean—she always was a clean lady."

"But the horse—what else did it tell you?" said Mabry's chief deputy, the twinkling-eyed Fred Bankston.

"That you'll be sheriff someday, if one of your wisecracks doesn't poison you," was Mabry's riposte.

"Well that horse told me something," Bankston had persisted, "if you don't mind me askin' questions of that horse of yours. I reckon that Miss Cynthia's no crazy killer. She's mighty particular what she serves her customers, and I'm thinking that she's been eating the sort of dish that's best served cold. And one more thing—something that the horse didn't tell me—I hear that young Ensor, way out in Texas, has sent something mighty pertinent to Jimmy Dobbs, son of the late lamented Delroy."

Which had made Sheriff Mabry think—then, and now as he swung back and forth on his porch—that Fred Bankston was a smart young man; and that barring accidents he would indeed be sheriff someday. He rounded out his post-dinner musings with two memories and one decision.

The memories were of how, obeying his summons, the Kinsors had come into Midville, driven by the ubiquitous Ed Raye, so Cynthia could be arrested. And how J.P., following Mabry's suggestion, had gone out to have a word with Ambrose McKye, who had agreed to take the case for $25, much less than his usual fee. And as for Mabry's decision, well, the sheriff was a fair-minded man. That Ensor package—might be something, might be nothing. He decided to advise Bankston to make inquires, before Jimmy Dobbs got around to destroying it.

19

Trial: The First Day

An air of expectancy pervaded the town of Midville on December 9, 1907, an air of anticipated revelation: a sense that long-buried secrets were about to be unlocked. The wood-framed courthouse, long weathered for lack of fresh paint, stood gray and bleak behind the one oak tree in the courtyard. The courthouse had been hastily built to replace the original one, which had burned at the turn of the century and, as a result of the haste, had been poorly planned and shabbily built.

The Probate Judge, Tax Assessor, and other county officers had office space on the first floor. The second floor was occupied by the county attorney with a small office reserved for the Circuit Judge when Circuit Court was in session. The remainder of the second floor was occupied by a courtroom and the adjacent jury room. The courtroom seated a hundred or so spectators on long wooden benches.

Although the courthouse clock had barely struck eight o'clock, spectators were already claiming seats. The crops had been harvested, and there was no reason not to come into town for a real show! The courthouse grounds were already covered, mostly by mule-drawn wagons. Wagon or automobile, most vehicles contained a covered basket of food. After all, Midville's one lone cafe could accommodate only a small part of the multitude of visitors.

At half past eight, Circuit Judge Raymond Holdbrook was seen entering a side door. Five minutes later county attorney Urban Kirksey entered the same door. At almost the same time, Ambrose McKye entered the front door and made his way up the stairs to the courtroom.

Attorney Kirksey was unusually excited, so hopeful that he would win, so much inflated with anticipation that he greeted McKye with a leering, smug expression. He was winless in every case he had been opposed by McKye. But in spite of his hopeful confidence, Kirksey sensed that this trial was going to be unusual; that there was some facet of truth yet to be unveiled. He had labored long hours in preparation and thought he knew the answer to each question he would ask the various witnesses. But a small, but nagging doubt remained. Had he considered and planned for all possibilities?

Ambrose McKye wore his habitual detached expression, but he, too, had nagging doubts about what he was about to do. He had conducted a long—redundantly long— research of all the facts of this case. He had conducted intensive interviews with Cynthia and James Kinsor. He had delved so deeply into each of their lives that he felt that he knew them better than they knew themselves. And to assure that they both knew and understood what he proposed to do, he had composed an affidavit confirming and agreeing to his proposal. Both signed it and McKye's secretary, a notary public, had authenticated it. To avoid possible leaks of the plan, he had waited until the day prior to the trial to reduce it to writing. So much for strategy. For tactics he could rely on a thorough knowledge of his neighbors' beliefs, their code of behavior, and likely reactions. And of course, on his knowledge of Raymond Holdbrook and Urban Kirksey. He was ready and able to fence with both of them, to keep Kirksey slashing away in the dark, until it was time to launch his counterattack. Lord knows it would be best, he told himself, if it comes as a surprise to the prosecution!

Now as the onset of the trial was imminent, both attorneys were introspective, both anxious. A tense hush had come over the courtroom. Spectators were standing in the aisles, and some were sitting in the open windows. Wash Mabry and Cynthia and James Kinsor entered and made their way to the defense table. Urban Kirksey was seated at the prosecution table. The court stenographer sat alertly in front of the bench, pad and pencils at the ready.

Precisely as the courthouse clock began tolling the hour of nine, the court bailiff appeared in the judge's office door. He stepped several feet into the courtroom and in a loud voice proclaimed: "All rise! Hear ye, all who have business before this honorable court, draw near and ye shall be heard! The Circuit Court of Chufenee County is now in session, the honorable Judge Raymond Holdbrook presiding." The judge entered and mounted the bench, and preparatory to sitting down himself, said: "Please be seated."

Holdbrook was very circumspect in performing his judicial duties. He hated surprises. His very nature demanded orderly process. He was impeccably dressed in white shirt, dark tie, and navy blue suit. His shoes were spit-shined. His hair was close-trimmed and neatly groomed. To those who did not know him, he appeared foppish. But he was no fop; he was tough-minded, and mentally acute. His professional pride was such that he would readily chastise any attorney whose court conduct indicated poor trial preparation or disrespect to his court. He was deeply religious and always engaged himself in a session of meditation before each day of court.

Those who knew Judge Holdbrook by reputation considered him the very personification of justice. If he had a flaw, it was that he had invested his ego, his very being, in his position. He loved the deference that others showed him, their eager interest in his slightest opinion, and to keep that elevated status he would—well, sometimes without strictly being aware of it, he would rule with an eye to the next election.

As he sat down, his eyes swept the scene before him: the overflow of spectators; the defense table with attorney McKye, Cynthia and James Kinsor; the prosecution table where county attorney Kirksey sat with his stack of papers; the court stenographer who seemed lost in some anticipatory world; and the bailiff who had seated himself between the opposing sides. Having satisfied himself that all was in good order, he raised his voice and asked: "Are all parties ready to proceed with this trial?"

The prosecutor rose to his feet and answered, "Urban Kirksey for the people, your honor."

Defense counsel rose to his feet and said, "Ambrose McKye for the defense. We are ready, your honor."

The judge then delivered a statement, which he spoken so often that to him it had become a normal routine. He began, with steely emphasis on each point, his accent somewhat nasal and Appalachian: "This court will at no time permit outbursts of emotions from the audience. The attorneys, Mr. Kirksey and Mr. McKye will not engage in leading or fishing-type questions. Your questions will be relevant to evidentiary information that is useful to the court and to the jury."

He paused to let these points sink in, poured a glass of water from a jug at his elbow, and continued: "Understandably, this is an emotional occasion, but emotions play no part in the search for truth, nor in the administration of justice. Now that we understand the rules of decorum, we must proceed to select a jury panel. Each side has been furnished with the *venire* of prospective jurors, a list Sheriff Mabry assures the court contains only names of those persons who are legally qualified for jury service. I now ask each attorney if he is ready to select a jury panel."

From Urban Kirksey, "I am, your honor." From Ambrose McKye, "I am, your honor." Then the judge continued: "You will each select six jurors, and each of you may exercise three removals for cause. We will now proceed with the jury selection."

At this instant, Ambrose McKye stood and addressed the court, "Your honor, I have carefully reviewed this list and find only one or possibly two names I would find objectionable. I therefore leave to the prosecution the selection of the entire panel. However, I would appreciate the court letting me keep my removals for cause."

Judge Holdbrook looked to attorney Kirksey, "What say you, Counselor?"

The prosecutor was taken aback at this turn of events and it showed on his face. He had to wonder if this was one of McKye's ruses. But he was given little time for such speculations.

"Mr. Kirksey, you are wasting the court's time."

"I concur," said Kirksey. "This is highly irregular, but I will choose the entire panel."

Kirksey picked up the list of prospective jurors and rapidly read twelve names. So fast was his reading that it was apparent that a part of his meticulous preparation was to choose, in advance, jurors who would be most apt to render a guilty verdict.

The judge and Ambrose McKye followed the selection with intense interest. At the finish, the judge stated that the selected panel was satisfactory to the court. He noted that the court clerk had administered a questionnaire in advance to each person in the venire. The cardinal question had concerned the individual's willingness to impose capital punishment upon conviction. Each of the selected jurors had indicated that he would be so willing.

He then asked, "Mr. McKye, do you object to any named individual on the proposed panel?"

Ambrose McKye quickly thought over the list. He knew each of the twelve men by reputation. All were good citizens, and at least three were particularly honorable: Micah Jordan, who ran the stables owned by his older brother Jeff; Richard Reeves, an up-and-coming farmer in the White's Gap community; and Harold Hollingsworth, an 1898 War veteran and noted breeder of livestock. McKye answered: "No, your honor, all of these men are honest, upright individuals. The defense accepts each person without objection."

"Very well, Mr. McKye. Now the clerk of the court will seat the jury panel and administer the oath of office."

As the jurors walked somewhat hesitantly from the spectators' seats to the jury box, the clerk stood in front of them. He waited until all were seated, asked them to stand with upraised right hands. He then read them the following oath:

"Do you solemnly swear that you will serve this honorable court as juror in the case of the State vs. Cynthia Kinsor; that you will consider only that evidence which is relevant to this case, as is deemed by this court; that you will cast your vote as guilty or as innocent, based solely on admitted evidence, without bias, free from whatever emotions you may feel, so help you God. If you so swear, say I do."

The panel in unison: "I do."

The judge then established the following rules of conduct for all members of the court.

"The jury panel will be sequestered until a verdict is rendered in this case. They will receive all meals at the Elite Cafe and they will be domiciled as a panel at the New Midville Hotel. Jurors will not read newspapers; they will not discuss their case among themselves outside the jury room; and no alcoholic beverages will be permitted them for the duration of this trial. And officers of this court are admonished not to speak to or release any trial information to any person or institution. Violation of this direction will result in a contempt citation for the offender."

Having issued that edict, the judge looked at his watch and promptly announced a recess until two o'clock.

Court reconvened promptly at two o'clock. The first item on the agenda was the reading of the indictments by the court clerk. The first two indictments were identical except for the names of the victims. In essence, they stated that Cynthia Kinsor did, on stated dates, with malice aforethought, cause the death of Alfred H. Ensor and Delroy Dobbs at or near the Springs five miles north of the town of Midville, by selling them each a quantity of corn whiskey, into which she had introduced an unknown poisonous substance which wrought powerfully upon their bodies with fatal effects. The third indictment was essentially the same except the charge was for the attempted murder of Lemuel Emerson.

The jurors listened intently as the clerk read the charges. Several of them were observed looking at the figure of Cynthia Kinsor as she sat very still, her poke bonneted head drawn down as if she were extremely shy. Her face was so completely hidden that no observation of her expression was possible.

Judge Holdbrook sat quietly, almost stoically, looking at the jury. He appeared to be gathering his thoughts and arranging them systematically. Then he began his remarks to the panel.

"I need not remind you of the gravity of the task you are about to undertake. We have here a citizen of your county who is charged with not one, but three heinous crimes. To make the case more difficult for you is the fact that the accused is a woman. I have never presided over a murder trial where a woman was the accused, and I have researched the criminal records of your county to determine if, in the history of the county, a woman had ever been charged with murder. The records reveal this is indeed the first such trial in the county. This court and you are therefore obligated to perform a duty that is at the outset onerous to the extreme. Men of the South are by nature and by breeding conditioned always to give our women folk the benefit of any doubt. But we are a nation ruled by law, and the law dictates that a jury's verdict must result from evidentiary findings. A court trial is a search for truth: truth untainted by dubious testimony, truth unmitigated by emotion, and truth undiluted by compassion for the victim or the accused. The law does not recognize social standing; it does not recognize financial holdings; it does not recognize gender. Law in its purest sense is totally dispassionate; is relentless in the pursuit of truth; and is impartial in administering justice. In this court that is the only way we will operate."

The judge continued: "Now, concerning the crimes the accused is charged with committing: there is no recourse to murder. It is an act of finality. It cannot be undone. It cannot be atoned for. No amount of regret can recall a murdered person to life. There is only the crime, followed by punishment upon conviction. I instruct you to keep these remarks in mind as you hear the evidence and as you render your verdict. . . . "I now ask the attorneys if they are ready for opening statements. Mr. Kirksey?"

"I am ready, your honor," said the prosecutor, whose expression betrayed his pleasure at Judge Holdbrook's remarks. Shuffling some notes on the table, spreading them out for convenient perusal,

Kirksey was evidently ready to launch into his opening—when Ambrose McKye rose easily to his feet, announcing: "The defense will have no opening statements, your honor."

Prosecutor Kirksey stared at his opponent in disbelief. He was now convinced that the defense attorney was up to one of his well-known departures from routine; and if the purpose of the announcement was to produce nervous doubt in the prosecution, it was admirably effective. With no opening statement from the defense, the prosecution was denied any knowledge of how the defense would be conducted. This only added to Kirksey's discomfort and doubt. His witness list contained a goodly number of credible (and, he admitted to himself, one or two less-credible) persons who had knowledge of the case. He was convinced that the testimony of persons on the list would prove guilt beyond a reasonable doubt. But still there was the lingering unease, the shadowy sense of impending failure, the eternal memory of trials lost to Ambrose McKye. Such were the flashbacks of Kirksey's mind.

The prosecutor shifted his gaze to Judge Holdbrook, who may have been indulging in similar memories of Prosecutions Lost. The two men looked at each other, and Holdbrook felt a stab of sympathy for the county's lawyer. Somewhat to his own surprise, he rescued Kirksey. Elaborately consulting his watch, the judge announced: "The hour is not late, but the day has been long. Court is recessed until nine o'clock tomorrow morning."

20
Trial: Morning, Second Day

Court reconvened promptly at nine o'clock on December 10. Again the courtroom was packed with spectators. The jurors were seated in two lines facing both the judge and the opposing sides. Cynthia Kinsor was seated between Ambrose McKye and her husband. Her appearance was the same as yesterday: elongated poke bonnet, Mother Hubbard dress and plain black, low-heeled shoes. Her demeanor was meek and unassertive. With her constantly bowed head, she was a picture of patient meditation.

The judge entered, nodding to the bailiff, whereupon that dignitary stood and shouted: "All rise!" Everyone stood as he recited his familiar litany; but courtroom noise continued for several seconds, causing the bailiff to declare in a louder voice, "Order in the court!" Spectators became quiet immediately.

The judge seated himself, then turned his attention to prosecutor Kirksey. "Mr. Kirksey, you may present your opening statement." Kirksey arose and solemnly addressed Judge Holdbrook and the jury. "Your honor and gentlemen of the jury, the people have indicted Cynthia Kinsor with two counts of first degree murder and one count of attempted murder. More specifically, the charges allege that on the twenty-ninth of July, 1906, she, with carefully planned malice, did sell to Alfred Ensor a scant pint of corn whiskey into which she had added a substance, as yet unidentified, which poisoned Mr. Ensor, causing his death. The second charge of murder is identical to the first, except for the victim. He was Delroy Dobbs, who was murdered on the second of March, 1907. The charge of attempted murder concerns the attempt, by Cynthia Kinsor, on the seventeenth of October, 1907, to murder Lemuel Emerson by the same method. How she failed will be proven by eyewitness testimony by Mr. Emerson. The people plead that you will be open-minded and objective in your deliberation in spite of the fact that the accused is a woman. She has always been a mysterious person to her friends and neighbors—someone who, for whatever dark reasons, didn't choose to share in the life of the community. Perhaps this trial will shed some light on *her* life."

Ending on this note of sarcasm, Kirksey turned to face Judge Holdbrook and said: "That is all, your honor."

"Very well, Mr. Kirksey. Since the defense has no opening statement, you may call your first witness."

"The prosecution calls Lemuel Emerson," said Kirksey.

"Lemuel Emerson to the witness stand," shouted the bailiff.

An old man, stooped and with the hesitant walk of old age, Emerson emerged from the witness room. Making his way to the witness stand, he surveyed the courtroom scene in a long, sweeping glance, finally coming to rest on Cynthia Kinsor. He paused, trying to comprehend her silent strength, her quiet stillness, for she neither moved nor looked in his direction. Spectators could tell that something was wrong; they put it down to the force of distressing memories. But the truth was that as Emerson came before the

presence of the woman he was about to accuse, he was overwhelmed by a sense of foreboding—a feeling that his appearance as
a witness against her was not in his best interest. Though his memories of that day last October were indeed fresh in his mind, he had
never actually seen her face, so carefully had she worn her long
sided poke bonnet. Her stoic acceptance, meek only in appearance
was, to him confusing and upsetting.

He advanced to the witness stand, was given the oath by the
court clerk, and took his seat.

Urban Kirksey stood to one side of the witness stand, assuring
that the judge had a clear view of and could hear the testimony.

Preliminary to the actual testimony, the prosecutor command-
ed, "State your name for the record."

"Lemuel Emerson," the witness obeyed.

"Mr. Emerson, what is your occupation?"

"I was a farmer."

"Now, Mr. Emerson, this trial is concerned with events which
occurred on October 17 of this year. Please relate to the court and
the jury exactly what happened to you, where it happened and the
person or persons involved."

To which Emerson gave his recitation, breathing, as he got
deeper into his narration, shorter and faster:

"I drove my buggy from my home in the Sand Valley Community to Midville, in order to conduct some—some business. I stopped
on the way at Eau Claire Springs. I stopped at the Kinsor home
which is situated on a knoll about a couple of hundred yards from
the spring. I pulled up by the gate and spoke to J.P. Kinsor, who was
seated on the porch. I told him I wanted to buy a bottle of whiskey.
Mr. Kinsor called to his wife and told her what I wanted. After some
minutes, Mrs. Kinsor appeared from a back room; the two walked to

the gate, handed me a pint bottle. I paid up and departed. I stopped at the springs for water for my horse and myself. While there I decided to take a drink. I swallowed a small amount. It tasted odd. I smelled the bottle. I tried to climb back up into the seat; but I felt dizzy. I fell off. I must have lost consciousness, how long I can't say, but at some point I came to—I seem to've felt a presence. I opened my eyes; I saw Cynthia Kinsor—saw her in a bonnet, like that one she's wearing now. She was standing with her hands on her hips, looking down at me. She was making a noise—she may have been breathing hard; she may have been laughing. I must have twitched. Anyway, I sat up; she hurried away. I could hear her running. I was on the ground for a long time. When I was able to get into the buggy, I drove into Midville, and stopped in at Dr. Peterson's. When I got a little better I saw Sheriff Mabry. I gave him the whiskey bottle and told him what had happened. He said he would investigate. That is the all I know."

"I have this further question," said Kirksey. "Are you positive the person at the spring was Cynthia Kinsor?"

"Yes, sir! There is no doubt in my mind."

The prosecutor turned to the judge and announced, "No further questions for this witness, your honor."

"Very well, counselor," said the judge. He then addressed Ambrose McKye: "Your witness."

McKye slowly rose from his chair, and with a quizzical expression on his face, approached the witness. "Mr. Emerson, you have stated under oath to this court that you are positive that you were poisoned by Cynthia Kinser; that she stood over you laughing; that she ran away when you stirred; and, oh yes, that your attacker was wearing a poke bonnet. Is that a fair summary of your testimony?"

"Yes, sir."

"Did you see your attacker's face?"

"Well, no."

"Then the person you encountered at the springs may not have been Cynthia Kinsor. She could have been any woman who was dressed like Cynthia Kinsor. Isn't that correct?"

"I don't think so; who else could it have been?"

"Mr. Emerson, this is a court of law, not one of personal opinions. I ask you again, are you positive that the person whom you say attempted to kill you was the defendant in this case, and do you now admit that there is a basis for doubt in your testimony?"

Before Emerson could answer, Urban Kirksey was on his feet addressing the judge. "Objection, your honor! The witness can answer only one question at a time. Counsel has posed two questions in one sentence."

"The objection is sustained," said the judge. "Counsel will restate the first question and allow the witness to answer. He will then pose the second question so the witness can answer. Proceed, Mr. McKye."

"Thank you, your honor. Now Mr. Emerson, are you positive the person who attempted to kill you was Cynthia Kinsor?"

Again Kirksey was on his feet. "The question has already been asked and answered."

"Sustained," said the judge. "Defense counsel will avoid repeat questions."

"Very well, your honor. I apologize to the court. Now Mr. Emerson, since you admit that you could not see the person's face, is there any doubt in your mind as to your positive identification of the defendant?"

Kirksey was silent; Emerson looked at his hands. He shifted in his chair, and without looking at anybody, said haltingly, "I don't think I have any doubt about it."

McKye sensed that indeed there was doubt in Emerson's mind. He pressed this advantage further by asking: "Did the person who attacked you say anything?"

"No, sir."

"Then that person could possibly have been a man. Is that a true statement?"

"I suppose so."

"Then you really have no idea who that person was?"

Emerson stirred in his seat: "Yes, I do! She was Cynthia Kinsor."

McKye turned abruptly and addressed Judge Holdbrook. "I have no further questions for this witness, your honor."

The judge then instructed the prosecutor to call his next witness.

"I call Henry Jones to the stand."

The bailiff opened the witness waiting room door, and announced, "Henry Jones to the stand." There was no movement from any one of the dozen or so witnesses-to-be. After a prolonged pause, he said, "Tanglefoot, come on!"

"Well howdy, Bailiff! I thought you was a callin' somebody else. I ain't heard my first name since Buck was a calf, and he's a full-growed bull now," said Jones.

"Get yourself in there right now," ordered the bailiff.

"You got it," said Jones as he waddled his way into the courtroom. His expression suddenly changed to that of a pleased grin. He stopped and slowly surveyed the audience, his eyes finally focusing on Urban Kirksey. He extended his hand to the prosecutor and greeted him with, "Howdy Mr. Urbie. How you?"

"Take the witness stand," hissed Kirksey under his breath.

Jones was then sworn and seated on the witness stand. The prosecutor approached him and began to question him.

"Where were you on the date of March 2, 1907?"

"I don't know."

"Were you at any time on that date at Eau Claire Springs?"

"Yup."

"Will you please tell the court what you were doing at the Springs?"

"I 'as passed out drunk, mostly."

"During those times when you were conscious, what did you see?"

"Nothin' much. I'd bought my whiskey, 'n I bad wanted to drink it."

"Did you see any other people there?"

"Yup."

"Who did you see?"

"I seen Mr. Delroy Dobbs and somebody in a long dress and a poke bonnet"—here he dropped his voice and looked at the spectators before saying theatrically—"the longest poke bonnet I ever seen. Finally I seen Mr. Ed Raye."

"What were they doing?"

"He 'as in my fav'rit spot! Least I thought he 'as passed out drunk, and he had my spot! But there was this woman 'as standin' by and lookin' down on him."

"Who was 'he'? Mr. Dobbs?"

"Yup."

"What else did you see?"

"The woman stepped back quick and left."

"What happened then?"

"I tried t' wake Mr. Dobbs—I nudg'd him onc'st or twic'st—I seen he weren't breathin'—then I went to get Mr. Ed Raye. Mr. Ed came down, tuk it all in, and sent me off to git the sheriff."

"Anything else?"

"I gave Mr. Ed the sheriff's message. He took hisself off to raise some neighbors, and I went back to watchin' the corpse."

Kirksey was ready to conclude Jones' testimony; but as he turned to give the witness over to McKye, Tanglefoot couldn't resist one more provocation.

"Ain't you gonna ask me what happened next?"

"That's not important," Kirksey said in a repressive tone. Then abruptly: "Your witness, Mr. McKye."

Amused by the spectacle of the prosecutor trying to hush his own witness, the defense attorney approached the witness stand, and asked, sympathetically: "What did happen next, Tanglefoot?"

"Mr. Ed went to J.P. Kinsor's house 'n bought me anuther pint. I drunk it; after that I can't remember."

One of the jurors shifted in his chair, a disgusted expression on his face. In a bland and gossipy voice, McKye continued: "Now Mr. Jones, you are employed at the Bigelow and Lewis saw mill. Is that correct?"

"Yup."

"And what is your job?"

"I off-bear the mill."

"Please explain to the court what 'off-bear' means."

"I hand-take the lumber from the saw-kerridge to the edger."

Urban Kirksey was on his feet. "Objection, your honor. Defense counsel's questions have no connection to this case. It does not matter how the witness earns his living!"

To which McKye replied, "I beg the court's patience, your honor. This line of questions goes to the credibility of the witness."

"You may proceed, Mr. McKye, but please get to the point. The objection is overruled for the time being."

"Thank you, your honor. Now Mr. Jones, you say you were drinking at Eau Claire Springs on the date in question, and that you were looking for a place in which to pass out; and that you saw Mr. Dobbs and a person who was wearing a long poke bonnet, and that person was in the bushes near Mr. Dobbs. Why were you at the Springs in the first place?"

"I had bought sum whiskey from Mrs. J.P. Kinsor, and when I got to the Springs, I began drinking."

"And you eventually passed out?'

"Uh-huh."

"Where were the two people whom you claim to have seen when you approached the Springs?"

"They 'as behind a clump of bushes."

"So you could not clearly see Mr. Dobbs and this other person?"

"I guess not, not t' first."

"Now, back to your job at the saw mill; when are you paid?"

"I get paid ever' Saturday morning."

"And on the day of your passing-out at the Springs, you had been paid that morning. Is that correct?"

"Yeah."

"And after you were paid, you went directly to the Kinsor house and bought a jar of corn whiskey?"

"Yeah."

"And you left the Kinsor house and went to the springs. Why?"

"I wanted some water to keep the whiskey from burning my mouth."

"And how much whiskey did you drink before you arrived at the Springs?"

"Most 'uv it."

"Nearly a whole jar?"

"Yup."

"And how much time passed from when you started drinking and when you had finished that jar?"

"I 'on't know."

"What time of day was it?"

"I 'on't know."

"What time was it when you saw Mr. Dobbs and this person in the poke bonnet?"

"Hell, I 'on't know. I ain't got no watch!"

At which point, Judge Holdbrook said to the witness: "You will not use profanity in this court! Do you understand?"

"Nope."

Attorney McKye explained the judge's admonition by saying: "You must not cuss in court."

"Aw right."

Then McKye continued his questioning. "Now Mr. Jones, you have testified under oath that you were at the Springs on the day in question; that you saw certain things; that you spent a period of time in a passed-out state; that you can't tell the court what time these things occurred; and that you saw whatever you saw through a clump of bushes. Is that a fair summary of your testimony?"

"I reckon so, though I did get close enuf to nudge the dead man."

"How did you feel after you drank that first pint?"

"My head was swimmin'."

"Could you walk straight?"

"Lord, no!"

"Was your vision clear?"

"As clear as it ever is."

"Now Mr. Jones, I invite your attention to the person sitting in the third row of seats from the front and in the seat on the aisle. Who is that person?"

The witness looked at the figure in the seat described by the attorney. He squinted, he peered and he fidgeted in his seat.

"That's Waldo Roberts."

The defense attorney walked to the aisle; placed his hand on the shoulder of the man in question. "Will you please stand and tell the court your name."

"My name is Cecil Abernathy."

"And what is your line of work?"

"I am the foreman at the Bigelow and Lewis saw mill."

"You are Mr. Jones' boss?"

"Yes, sir."

McKye turned to face the court. "Your honor, I have no further questions of the witness. He seems to have testified to his own lack of credibility."

"Very well, Mr. McKye," said the judge. "Mr. Kirksey, call your next witness."

Wincing a little, Kirksey said: "Thank you, your honor. I call Edward E. Raye to the witness stand."

Raye, a tall, craggy man, emerged from the witness room. The hair of this Sagacious Sophomore was unusually well-groomed. He was dressed in an old gabardine suit. He wore new brown brogan shoes and walked with something of a shuffle. His gaze was a piercing stare out of steel blue eyes. His entire demeanor was that of laid-back curiosity mixed with a hint of boredom. He was sworn and seated in the witness chair.

From the prosecutor: "Please state your name."

"Edward Elroy Raye." He rolled out these syllables clearly; he was a man who loved words, and maybe loved wordplay even better.

"Where do you live, Mr. Raye?"

"I reside on Lovejoy Road at the top of the hill by Eau Claire Springs."

"You own the farm next to Eau Claire Springs, is that correct?"

"I own the legal right to occupancy."

"Does that mean you rent the farm?"

"No. It means that I have a deed through which the state grants me the right to occupy and enjoy the products of the land."

"As you please. Now how is your house situated with regard to the springs?"

"It is atop the hill overlooking the springs."

"Then you have a clear view of the entire pond which is formed by the flow of the springs; is that correct?"

"The lagoon, or perhaps the bayou. Yes."

"Now on the day and the hour of the attempted murder of Mr. Emerson by the defendant, where were you?"

"I was on my front porch, reading a daily periodical."

Kirksey wondered how this polyphonic music was playing with the jury. Two or three of them were smiling, he noticed. He asked: "Please tell the court what you saw and heard from the area of the springs."

"I heard nothing. I saw the legs and feet of a man lying on the ground in a clump of bushes, with a female figure standing near him. And I saw another man making his approach."

"With regard to the female figure, what was she doing?"

"That, I don't know. She was still, apart from some movement of her arms. Beyond that I have no idea"—Raye spoke more slowly—"no definitive concept."

"Can you tell the court how the female figure was dressed?"

"All I can say is that she was appareled in a poke bonnet and a long dress."

"Can you identify that person in this courtroom today?"

"No."

"Could it have been Cynthia Kinsor?"

"Possibly."

Kirksey thought he saw an opening: "Then we can assume that it was Cynthia Kinsor?"

Attorney McKye rose to his feet and shouted, "Objection, your honor! Assumption and possibilities should not be considered in the administration of justice."

"The objection is sustained," stated Judge Holdbrook, severely. "Mr. Kirksey, you surely know better!"

"I apologize, your honor. I have no more questions. Your witness."

"No questions, your honor," responded McKye. The judge then consulted his watch, and announced: "Court is adjourned until two o'clock."

J.P. spoke a few encouraging words—the best he could do—to Cynthia, and began walking back to lawyer McKye's house for lunch. On the way, he was hailed by a black child whom he recognized as Joe Will Dowdell, son of Midville's Tuskegee-trained cobbler. Keeping pace with J.P.'s peculiar gait, Joe Will announced: "I wuz to tell Mr. Kinsor that if he ever needed to shift from here quick, he should git word to the barber shop."

Still thinking over the morning's events, J.P. mumbled that Midville had no barber shop, to which Joe Will replied, before running off: "Send for Mr. Nate back of Jordan's Sto'."

Wheels were beginning to turn in J.P.'s mind, but he was too preoccupied to thank Joe Will. For the moment he filed the information away as something that he would figure out when this awful trial was over.

21
Trial: Afternoon, Second Day

After lunch, once the courtroom had settled down, Judge Holdbrook asked Urban Kirksey to call his next witness.

He responded: "I call Sheriff Washington Mabry to the stand."

The sheriff was brought into the courtroom and duly sworn. His hair had recently been cut and he was wearing a suit and tie—not his usual appearance.

"Now Sheriff Mabry, you arrested the accused on October 22, 1907. Is that correct?"

"Not exactly. I sent word to her and she came to the jail voluntarily."

"Nonetheless, she has been confined to jail since that date, hasn't she?"

"She's been in my custody since that date. Our county jail is no fit place to confine a woman. I have therefore kept her in my house since the day of the events at the springs."

For all his preparation, Kirksey had not done much conferring with Mabry. Now he wished he had. Nonetheless he decided to trust to his luck. He told himself that, he was an experienced lawyer, and he had been a debater since his days at the Academy—a pretty good one, he thought. Surely his forensic skills would put him on the same level, in the jury's eyes, with the stolid man on the witness stand—his witness, after all! He asked: "Now Sheriff, is it your custom to give such *preferential* treatment to persons accused of such *heinous* crimes as is the accused in this case?" He swept his eyes over the jury—doubtless, they would have no sympathy for a murderess—and caught a glimpse of the Reverend Mr. Amos, sitting among the spectators. Rev. Mike nodded emphatic approval.

Mabry simply observed: "It is my custom to treat all prisoners in a humane manner if their behavior and reputation deserve it. Mrs. Kinsor has been a model of behavior at all times. In fact, she has helped Mrs. Mabry prepare meals for the other prisoners. She has asked for no favors; nor has she been granted special privileges."

"During the time she has been in your custody, what have you learned as to evidence of her guilt?"

"Nothing."

Once more Kirksey was shaken. Whose side was the sheriff on? Once more the debater, he asked: "Nothing, Sheriff?"

"Nothing."

Kirksey, incredulously: "Did you try to gain information from her or any other of the principals in this case?"

"Not really. Mr. Emerson related to me the same information contained in his testimony. And I know better than to try to question the accused or any of the others in the case."

"Why not?"

"For one reason, Mrs. Kinsor speaks very few words about anything. Her husband and her neighbors are tight-lipped most times. I knew they would tell me nothing. Why should they?"

Kirksey turned toward the jury, more in sorrow than in anger: "Then is it fair to say you exerted little, if any, effort to learn the truth about the events of July 29, 1906, March 2, 1907, and October 17, 1907?"

"You could say that. I know the witnesses in this case. They are mostly good people"—this with a shrug as he thought of Tanglefoot Thomas. He continued: "They will tell the truth. You will get the truth directly, not filtered through me."

Again Kirksey looked toward the jurors, one of whom refused to meet his glance. There were several additional questions that he might have asked, but this lawman had thrown him off balance. So he contented himself with: "Sheriff Mabry, I sincerely hope you are correct!"

The prosecutor then turned to attorney McKye and said: "Your witness."

McKye stood and said to the judge, "I have no questions for this witness, your honor."

"Call your next witness, Mr. Kirksey," directed the judge.

Prosecutor Kirksey called to the witness stand James Emmitt Dobbs, a middle-aged man who was the son of the deceased Delroy Dobbs. He was sworn and took the stand.

"For the record: "You are the only son of Delroy Dobbs?"

"Yes."

"We know that your father was found dead at Eau Claire Springs, and we also know that at the time, the coroner could not determine the exact cause of his demise. He did determine that a half-empty scant pint of corn whiskey was suspected of containing some substance other than whiskey. I now ask you if your father was subject to seizures of any sort, the result of which was a state of unconsciousness."

"No, sir."

"Not ever?"

"Not to my knowledge."

"Did you ever witness your father's purchase of whiskey from the defendant?"

"Yes."

"Previous to March of this year, did he ever experience a loss of consciousness from drinking whiskey purchased from the defendant?"

"No. My father was an occasional drinker. He never drank enough to become drunk."

"Did your father ever comment on the quality of whiskey produced by the defendant?"

"Yes. He often stated that it was some of the best whiskey he could find without going out of the county. Sometimes, he got his whiskey by mail."

Kirksey paused for a long moment. Then: "Where were you when you learned that your father had been murdered?" he asked.

Attorney McKye quickly interposed: "The defense objects to the allegation that Mr. Dobbs was murdered. There is no proof of murder."

"The objection is sustained," said the judge. "Mr. Kirksey, rephrase your question."

Kirksey hesitated, leafed through some notes, and continued: "When your father died, did you suspect that he had met with foul play?"

"No."

"Why not?"

McKye was instantly on his feet, and in an anguished voice asked: "Your honor, I must ask the purpose of this line of questioning. Neither whereabouts nor suspicions of this witness have any bearing on this case! The prosecution appears to be aimless with this witness."

Judge Holdbrook looked at Kirksey, perhaps reflecting on why this man had never won against McKye, and asked: "Indeed Mr. Kirksey, what is the relevancy of your last few questions?"

The prosecutor hesitated for several seconds, then replied: "Your honor, my purpose is to ask this witness what transpired during and after a conversation he had with Alfred Ensor's son a short time after the death of Mr. Delroy Dobbs."

"Then please get to the point, Mr. Kirksey. The court agrees that your last few questions have no apparent bearing on this case!"

"Very well, your honor."

"Now, James Emmitt, did John Roy Ensor come to the field where you were working, about a month after your father's death, and if so, can you tell the court what was said by each of you?"

James Emmitt Dobbs stared at his hands, and fidgeted—seemingly embarrassed, at a loss for words.

From the judge: "Mr. Dobbs, you have been asked a question. You are directed by the court to answer."

Finally James Emmitt blurted out: "Johnny Ensor told me that—that Kinsor woman had killed my Daddy—that she had killed his daddy, too! He wanted me to go with him to Sheriff Mabry and swear out a warrant!"

The prosecutor then asked: "Did he go and did you accompany him?"

"I didn't go that day. No sir."

"And why not?"

"I didn't think it could be true about Father. Besides, Mrs. Kinsor—the old woman in the poke bonnet? I couldn't believe—not then—that she was capable of murder! I didn't want to rake up Daddy's affairs."

"Did John Roy Ensor go to Sheriff Mabry as he threatened?"

"Not then, I think, but later he got back in touch with me."

"By that time, had anything caused you to see things differently?"

"Yes," said Dobbs. "When he first mentioned murder, I was so mad that I warned him off our land. Johnny pulled up stakes 'n left for Texas some weeks later—seemed like he was in a hurry once he made up his mind—and I haven't seen him since. But once the news spread about Mr. Emerson's poisoning, he must have gotten word. He sent me his father's notebook then, and asked me to show it to you."

"Do you recognize this book?" asked Kirksey, holding up what looked like the kind of store-bought diary that locks with a little brass key.

"Yes, that's it," Dobbs replied.

"Please read the first marked passage," Kirksey instructed, and Ensor read from the book's first page:

"Journal of Alfred Ensor, 1906.

"Now read the second marked passage."

"June 24, 1906. Drove to Midville. Horseshoes and harness repairs. Stopped at Eau Claire Springs—watered Bessie. Spoke with Cynthia Kinsor. Had sometimes bought whiskey from her and J.P.— but today the first time I ever looked at her good, and that by accident. Unnerving. Bad disfigurement. I seemed to see a flash of something else, too. Strange. Goose walking on my grave?"

"Now," said Kirksey, please read the next marked passage.

James Emmitt turned over the leaves carefully, found his place, and read: "July 14, 1906. Been thinking. Terrible doings then. Lem and DD. That girl. Dead? Preaching at church—Rev. Amos. Hell-fire—liars, hypocrites. No ice water in Hell! Want to talk about war's end. Not to Bro. Amos. Maybe one more look—to make sure."

James Emmitt's voice had faltered as he wandered through these cryptic statements. He was not a practiced reader, but some of the spectators perceived that his problem was something besides inexperience. Kirksey understood that he was reluctant, and in a kindly voice asked, "Now, if you'll just read one more passage. The last one, the one marked with a red ribbon."

Dobbs cleared his throat, and said: "July 28, 1906. No sleep. Must talk to someone. Dr. Jim-Joe? Won't mention D or L. Dirty bastards! Will drive to town tomorrow."

"What do you make of those passages, Mr. Dobbs?" asked the District Attorney.

"I don't rightly know," he replied after a pause. "It seems like he'd done somethin' bad and was worried about it."

Upon which Kirksey, displaying a rare judgment of the dramatic, turned to Judge Holdbrook and stated, "No further questions, your honor."

"Mr. McKye, you may examine the witness," stated the judge.

"Thank you, your honor, I have no questions for this witness," replied McKye. This reply, incidentally, went against all of McKye's professional instincts. Normally he would have hammered away at the notebook's ambiguity—even sown doubts as to its authenticity, dispatched as it was from a distant state. McKye, however, was determined to stick to his plan.

Judge Holdbrook then turned to the prosecutor and asked, "Mr. Kirksey, do you have other witnesses to examine at length?"

"No, your honor, not at length, but I do have one witness whose testimony should last no longer than a few minutes."

"Then call that witness now. Court will recess until tomorrow at nine o'clock immediately after the witness' testimony is complete."

"I call Effie Alexander," replied the prosecutor.

The county librarian was called from the witness room. She walked briskly to the witness stand, was sworn and sat down, composed and purposeful.

"Please state your name for the record," ordered the prosecutor.

"Effie Alexander," was the reply.

"You are employed by the county as librarian?"

"Yes, sir," she replied.

"Over the past decade, how many books has Cynthia Kinsor checked out?"

"Just one, and I have the library card for it," said the librarian, cutting straight to the point.

"What is the title?"

In measured tones Miss Alexander replied: "*Poisonous Snakes of the Southern United States.*"

"How often did she check it out?"

"At intervals," she said, looking over at the jury. "She checked it out twice in the fall of 1904 and twice more in 1906."

The prosecutor turned to the judge and stated: "That is all, your honor."

"Mr. McKye, you may cross examine," stated the judge.

"I have no questions for the witness, your honor," replied McKye.

"Then court is recessed until nine o'clock tomorrow morning," stated the judge.

22

Interlude: Client Conference

During the late afternoon of December 10, after court had recessed, Ambrose McKye and J.P. Kinsor visited Cynthia at Wash Mabry's home. The purpose of the visit was once more to discuss in detail their plans of procedure, to be put into play once the prosecution had finished presenting evidence. One of McKye's main concerns was that one or both of the Kinsors might be fearful of the outcome of his plan. Fearful of a guilty verdict, or fearful of stirring up trouble in the county.

"Do you both remain committed to our plan, and are you still convinced that despite the risks inherent in it, it is the best course of action?" asked McKye.

J.P.'s answer, after a brief hesitation, was "Yes." Cynthia nodded her assent.

McKye then predicted that the prosecution would present no other witnesses and that Urban Kirksey would rest the prosecution early the next day. "His case is strong in parts, but flimsy in others," he said. "I believe we have neutralized enough testimony to create

133

some doubt in the minds of most of the jury panel. But between 'some doubt' and 'reasonable doubt' there is a wide gap! Many a man sits in prison whose jurors had some doubts—but not enough to acquit."

Once more he gathered up the Kinsors with his eyes, and continued. "What we are proposing is to undermine what Judge Holdbrook told us all about 'truth.' We want the jurors to see beyond the surface truth, beyond fact-truth, to the underlying truths of this case." He paused, seeming to collect his thoughts, and looked up at the corner of Wash Mabry's parlor ceiling.

"We want to show them that there is more than one kind of truth at work in this, as in so many of the transactions of this fallen life!" Seeming to catch himself, McKye grinned and said, in a lower tone: "But maybe I should save my closing oration for the jury?"

Then, with sincere optimism in his voice, he said briskly: "I feel almost certain that Harold Hollingsworth will be elected foreman of the jury, and if that is the case, the deliberation will be orderly and fair. Now, J.P., come with me back to my house. Cynthia, I hope you won't have to stay with Wash and Mrs. Mabry too much longer. J.P. will come here in the morning and go with you and the sheriff to the courthouse. Under our plan you will both be testifying tomorrow. Until then, try to keep your spirits up and expect the best outcome."

Having satisfied himself that the Kinsors remained steadfast behind his plan of defense, McKye escorted J.P. Kinsor to his house, saw him settled in a guest bedroom, and then went to his office. He sat at his desk, hardly moving, until almost eight p.m. Ordinarily, he would have had before him several law books, reading first from one and then others, busily assembling authorities in preparation for tomorrow. But for the maneuver he was about to pull there was little or no case law. So all he could do was ponder his actions and the impression his witnesses would make on the jury, occasionally making a note on a blank page of his yellow legal pad. As the courthouse clock struck eight, he left his office, walked to his home and went to bed.

23
Trial: Morning, Third Day

When court opened next morning, as McKye had predicted, Kirksey informed the court that the prosecution rested.

As the prosecutor made the announcement, he cast a nervous glance toward the defense table. While he felt confident that he was winning the case, he still could not rid himself of the fear that McKye had some devious scheme yet to play. The feeling was well-grounded in historical fact.

Judge Holdbrook thanked the prosecutor and turned his attention to the defense. "Counselor McKye, if you are ready, you may call your first witness."

"Thank you, your honor. The defense calls Emmaline Clifton as our first witness." Heads turned among the spectators as J.P. and Cynthia's one-time savior, who might have been young once but was now (as one stage-whispering young woman put it) "pushing a hunnerd," walked in stately fashion toward the witness box.

Duly sworn, the venerable Miss Clifton slowly lowered herself into the witness chair.

Advancing briskly toward his witness, McKye asked her to identify herself. She stated in a clear if somewhat cracked voice: "I am Emmaline Clifton. I am a house-holder. I was a sometime midwife, en' I know a good deal about medicinal herbs."

"Now, Miss Clifton, what knowledge, if any, do you have of the accused in this case?"

"In the summer of 1865 I took Cynthia Kinsor into my home. She stayed on into the spring of 1866."

"What was the occasion or what was the reason for taking her into your home?"

"She had been severely beaten. She had been raped, en' she was as near death as was possible whilst still able to breathe. I had never seen a person so badly hurt as she was on the day I first saw her."

"How was she able to get to your house?"

"J.P. Kinsor brought her. She was tied across the back of J.P.'s mule. He told me he had discovered her lying in a pool of blood near the Springs."

"When she came to your home, was she conscious?"

"No."

"She was not conscious?"

"No."

"I mean, would you say she was unconscious?"

"Yes."

"How long was she that way?"

"She opened her eyes only after some weeks of lying in a stupor."

"Did she speak?"

"Not at first."

"When did she first speak?"

"She was able to say 'water' eventually."

"Now Miss Clifton, did you know Cynthia prior to her arrival at your home?"

"No."

"Did she tell you anything about her family, her childhood?"

"No."

"Has she ever told you her family's name?"

"No."

"Did you ask her?"

"Yes, many times."

"Do you have an opinion as to why she told you so little?"

"I didn't think she could remember. It was a miracle that she survived."

"Then how did you know that her first name was Cynthia?"

"She told me that much. It was all she could say, or would say, of her past life."

"So you have no clue as to the details of that life?"

"No."

"Now Miss Clifton, can you describe for the jury just what injuries Cynthia suffered?"

Prosecutor Kirksey stirred, got on his feet and shouted, "Miss Clifton is not a medical doctor, and is therefore not qualified to render an expert medical opinion. What do these matters have to do with the case? They're ancient history!"

McKye replied to the judge that he had not asked for an expert medical opinion—just a description of Cynthia's injuries. Then, with a shark's smile that he usually tried to keep off his face, he reminded the judge: "As to the relevancy of this line of questioning—Mr. Kirksey himself promised the jurors and this court that we should be learning about Mrs. Kinsor's secrets."

Judge Holdbrook hesitated momentarily, smiled dryly at the defense lawyer, and then ruled: "The objection is denied; but Mr. McKye, you should be somewhat more specific in how you frame your questions."

"I will do that, your honor," stated McKye.

Then turning to the witness, McKye instructed her: "Just tell the jury what you observed on the day you first saw Cynthia Kinsor."

"Her head en' shoulders were matted with dried blood. Both eyes were swollen shut. Her breathing was labored; her pulse was weak, irregular; she was very pale. Apparently both jaws were fractured, for her chin was pushed to the right side of her face, en' her nose appeared to have been smashed by a heavy blow."

McKye followed up, asking: "Was she fully dressed?"

"No. Her dress was torn at several seams en' she had no undergarments."

Now he spoke slowly: "Did you observe any other injuries on her body?"

"Yes. She was bleeding from—from her genitals."

The spectators shifted slightly at the use of this clinical term, unlady-like, but permissible from an elderly midwife. McKye drove home his point in a stern voice: "Did you at a later date have positive proof that she was indeed raped?"

"Yes."

"And what was that proof?" he asked, heralding the response that everyone, all at once, knew was coming.

"Nine months later, she gave birth to a baby boy."

"Miss Clifton, I ask you again. Has Cynthia Kinsor ever said or done anything which has led you to believe she can remember her full name?"

"No. If she knows, she has kept it to herself."

This ended McKye's questioning of Emmaline Clifton. He turned to Urban Kirksey and said: "Your witness."

Kirksey advanced to the witness, hesitated dramatically, and then began his cross-examination of Miss Clifton.

"Ma'am, you have stated that the accused stayed in your home from the summer of 1865 until she recovered enough to become ambulatory at or around the spring of 1866, is that correct?"

"Yes."

"During that time, what treatment and care did you provide her?"

"At first, I applied poultices en' hot towels to her face, en' fed her broth and pureed foods with a spoon. I discovered that, though she was unconscious, her swallowing reflex was partially active. I was able to feed her very carefully by letting the semi-liquids trickle from the spoon to the corner of her mouth, and thus to her throat. As the pap reached her throat, she would swallow. She would sometimes become strangled and cough. I had to be very careful not to let the materials get to her lungs. Ever so gradually she became better at swallowing, and at times I thought she was trying to cooperate in her feeding. But it was months before she was alert enough to feed herself, en' even longer before she took her first steps."

Kirksey had listened somewhat impatiently. Now he asked: "So you successfully nursed her back to life. Did she continue to live in your home?"

"She lived in my home until she was ready to leave."

"And where did she go when she left your home?"

"She went to J.P. Kinsor's home."

"Did she and Mr. Kinsor marry?" Here the jurors watched Kirksey's mouth prune up.

"I don't know," Miss Clifton said calmly. "I never asked."

Kirksey couldn't help himself: "Weren't you curious?"

At which time McKye rose to his feet and addressed the judge: "Your honor, I can see no connection between this case and the People's line of questions."

The judge replied: "Neither can I. Mr. Kirksey, get to the point of your cross-examination of the witness."

"Your honor, the questions go to establish the character of the accused," said Kirksey.

"I believe the character of the accused has been established by the fact that a duly-appointed grand jury has indicted her on two counts of premeditated murder and one count of attempted murder," was the judge's terse reply. Holdbrook was, thought McKye, batting for the prosecution even more openly than before; but he decided to let it go.

Kirksey, not quite understanding the gift he had been given, could not suppress the pouty tone in his response: "Then I have no further questions of this witness."

The judge looked at his watch and abruptly announced that court was recessed until one o'clock. It may have been, McKye observed under his breath to the Kinsors, the first time a judge ever gave a prosecutor time to recover his temper. "And the jury doesn't appreciate his courtesy at all," he added, looking over at Harold Hollingsworth.

24

Trial: Afternoon, Third Day

P romptly at one o'clock, Judge Holdbrook entered the court-room. The bailiff called: "Order in the court, all rise." The judge took his seat and said, "Please be seated."

He then addressed McKye, instructing him to call his next witness. "Thank you, your honor. I call J.P. Kinsor to the witness stand."

The aged, white-haired Kinsor limped into the courtroom, was sworn and took his seat. His weathered face reflected the continual pain from his crippled leg. His steel blue eyes were clear and steady. He sat with hands folded across his lap, his demeanor a study of stoic determination.

"Please state your name for the record," instructed McKye.

"James Polk Kinsor," stated the witness.

"How old are you, Mr. Kinsor?"

"I am sixty-three years of age."

Facing Kirksey's innuendos head-on, McKye asked, in his best courtroom voice: "You are the common-law husband of Cynthia Kinsor, the accused in this trial, is that correct?"

"Yes."

"You and she were never formally and legally married?"

"No."

And now more kindly, McKye asked: "How long have you lived together as man and wife?"

"For right about forty years."

"Miss Emmaline Clifton has testified that you discovered your wife at the Springs, and that you carried her to Miss Clifton's home and that she was very bloody from severe wounds to the face and head; that she was unconscious, and that both eyes were swollen shut. Is that the way you remember the occasion?"

"Yes." Kinsor's air was that of a man willing himself to remember. McKye persisted:

"Did you recognize her as any person you had ever known?"

"No, I had never seen her."

"So you did not know her name?"

"No."

"Has she ever told you her full name?"

Kinsor said, with an air of great simplicity: "No. Not until just the other day."

Now the spectators, almost as one, shifted in place and learned forward. The courtroom was quiet as McKye asked: "Had you ever asked her what her last name was?"

"Yes, many times."

"What have her answers been?"

"She said she couldn't remember."

"Did you believe her?"

Firmly: "Yes, for I had no reason to think otherwise."

"Now, Mr. Kinsor, you are a veteran of the Confederate Army. You suffered a leg wound at Gettysburg, a wound that has rendered you more or less disabled ever since. Is that correct?"

Kinsor bridled at the word "disabled," but replied: "Yes."

"Then how have you earned a living?"

"I get a pension from the state, and I help Cynthia make small crops of cotton and corn each year. We get by."

"Your wife makes a crop?"

"Yes, almost without help—and not only that, she makes a vegetable garden each year; and she chops wood for the cook stove and fireplace."

"Don't you think it odd for a Southern woman to do so much manual labor?"

Kinsor hesitated briefly, before saying, his voice slightly raised: "Of course it's unusual! But she's always insisted that she do it, because, she says, she owes me for her life."

McKye, now, getting down to brass tacks: "Has she ever by admission or implication indicated to you that she had anything to do concerning the allegations against her in this court?"

"No."

"Have you ever asked her if she was involved?"

"No."

"Why not?"

"She doesn't have much to say about anything. I know she would not tell me—or anybody else—something like that."

"Now Mr. Kinsor, I understand it is your practice to sit on your front porch when the weather permits. As you sit on your porch, can you see the Springs?"

"No. I can see the grove that stands around the Springs."

"Then you don't know if your wife was at the Springs on the date the state claims she attempted to kill Mr. Emerson?"

"No."

"Do you know whether she was at home on that date?"

"No."

McKye turned to Kirksey and said: "Your witness."

Kirksey hesitated briefly. He was far from being a complete fool. He might trip over his own nerves, sometimes, but he knew better than to assault such a perfect witness. Not to his face; better to do it in summation, if at all. He now addressed the judge "I have no questions for this witness, your honor."

"Very well," replied the judge. "Mr. McKye, call your next witness."

"Thank you, your honor. I call Cynthia Kinsor."

Another rustle of sound—the combined noise of more than a hundred persons shifting their positions on hard oak benches— greeted the defense attorney's announcement. All eyes were on the Mother Hubbard-clad figure as she slowly and deliberately stood and paced toward the witness stand. She was duly sworn and was directed to sit in the witness chair.

"Please state your name for the record."

Her small voice said: "Cynthia Kinsor."

"Are you the common-law wife of J.P. Kinsor?"

"Yes."

Members of the jury were leaning forward in an attempt to understand the words spoken, the sounds shaped and propelled by the tiny voice of the witness.

Noticing this, the judge instructed Mrs. Kinsor to speak louder.

"I can't," said the witness.

"Why not?" asked the judge.

"My vocal cords 'as injured," was the jagged reply.

McKye addressed the judge to suggest that since both he and the judge were close enough to hear and understand Cynthia's testimony, he, McKye, would repeat her answers to the jury. After a long moment the judge agreed, admonishing McKye to repeat her words precisely. To which the defense attorney had readily consented—both men having briefly eyed Urban Kirksey. The latter was at that moment busily scribbling notes, happy that he had avoided the trap of cross-examining J.P. Kinsor, oblivious to the advantage just seized by the defense. Another moment passed, without objection; then McKye, in a kindly and solicitous voice, said:

"Now Mrs. Kinsor, I am about to ask you some questions which may be embarrassing to you and which will revive memories which are painful in the extreme. For that I apologize to you and to your husband."

A silence that was almost a living entity had fallen over the courtroom. It was a silence of tension; a silence charged more by emotion than by anticipation. The mystery that shrouded Cynthia Kinsor had long been something of a legend to the public. In every way, she had been an enigma. Despite her quiet and timid demeanor, the mystery had wrapped itself about her past and had made her a local celebrity. Thus the occasion of her testimony was pregnant with all sorts of possibilities. It was that situation almost inconceivable in a small town—one, namely, in which nobody knew what to expect.

As the spectators sorted out their feelings, McKye continued: "You have lived as the wife of J.P. Kinsor for some forty years. Is that correct?"

"Yes."

"The witness' reply is 'yes.'" McKye addressed the jury, speaking that one word with an air of sincerity and good faith. Then, turning back to Cynthia Kinsor, he continued: "Prior to living with your husband, you lived at the home of Mrs. Clifton. Is that correct?"

"Yes."

"The witness' answer is 'yes,'" McKye repeated, this time keeping his eyes towards the witness stand. "Prior to living with Mrs. Clifton, where did you live?"

"With my family."

"The answer is 'With my family.'" McKye paused, and then continued, taking a step towards the audience: "And what was your family name?"

"Hedrick. My pa's name was Herman and my ma's name was Naomi."

"The witness states that her maiden name was Hedrick, her father's given name was Herman and her mother's given name was Naomi. Were there other family members, Mrs. Kinsor?"

"Yes, two brothers—Tom and Herman, Jr."

"The witness states that there were two brothers, Thomas and Herman, Jr. Do you remember any events which occurred to your family in the summer of 1865?"

"Yes."

"The answer is yes," McKye repeated immediately. "Will you tell the court exactly what happened to your family during the night of July 23, 1865?"

The bonneted figure leaned forward, speaking in short, breathy sentences. As she spoke her tiny voice projected itself past McKye, so that the jury and even the larger courtroom community could hear at least some pieces of it without the lawyer's assistance.

She began: "It was about nine o'clock. Ma and Pa was in bed. My brothers and I was in the parlor, playing a card game. The front door was open; left cracked open. All 't once those three—Alfred

Ensor, Delroy Dobbs, and Lemuel Emerson—crushed in. They had pistols; they commenced firing; shot my brothers sittin' down, who never even spoke. They went room to room and found my parents. Ma screamed; they shot 'em both. They tied me up and laid me on the floor. They carried the bodies out the back of the house, into a plowed field; they buried 'em. I found it later. A while later."

Catching her breath, Cynthia Kinsor continued: "They set fire to the house and barn. As the house fire flamed up, they tied me across the back of a horse and carried me to a thicket, near th' Springs. There they all—molested me. When they was done doing that, one of them smushed me in the face with the butt of his pistol. I must've passed out after the second lick, 'cause that's all I remember 'til I woke up 't Miss Effie's." At this point Cynthia's agitation was audible, and despite the poke bonnet, visible.

McKye then addressed the judge and said: "Your honor, I request a short recess. My client needs to recover her breath and composure. I further request that the testimony just given be transcribed by the court stenographer and a copy furnished to each juror, the prosecutor, the defense and the court. The statement of the witness is too long and too important for me to risk my memory in repeating it verbatim."

Once more, Judge Holdbrook assented, looking at the prosecutor—who looked up from his notes and nodded agreement.

The judge looked at his watch, hesitated a moment and announced: "The day has been long and tiresome. Court will be in recess until nine o'clock tomorrow."

25

Trial: Morning, Fourth Day

Many spectators remained in the courtroom. There was an immediate loud hum of conversation, all of it concerned with Cynthia Kinsor's testimony. They had only partially heard what she had said in answer to the defense attorney's last question. There were many murmured voices, asking: "What did she say? What?" to those who were seated on the front row of the seats.

Yet even the hard-of-hearing were aware that this strange woman had conjured something fearful from the past. Some of the spectators could be heard muttering about "wild justice," as their grandparents had called it—killing sprees, the bastard offspring of war. After a few minutes all the watchers, like minor players reluctant to leave the stage, slowly drifted out; and the courtroom became quiet.

Again J.P. Kinsor returned to Ambrose McKye's guest bedroom while Cynthia returned to Wash Mabrey's home. As usual, she helped Mrs. Mabrey prepare supper for the other prisoners. To all appearances, she had regained her inner calm; certainly she was silent as usual. J.P. spent a restless night. He feared what might happen the next day. There was an enduring bond of love and affection between the strange old couple—whatever Cynthia had done—and the thought that he might lose her to a prison term was a burden he was unprepared to bear. As for him: his advanced age was not in his favor. Many of his Confederate contemporaries were already dead. He often wondered to himself why and how he had survived so long. At four o'clock he finally sank into a fretful sleep.

He was up and dressed by seven o'clock on December 12. He limped to the jail yard and sat on the steps. Cynthia and Mrs. Mabrey were busily occupied in preparing breakfast for the jail inmates. From where he sat he could see the courthouse and the surrounding area. Wagons, buggies, and automobiles filled all available spaces. People were streaming toward the courthouse. Obviously word of Cynthia's testimony had spread quickly. Whatever the spectators had actually heard hardly mattered, for it had fueled rumors, which had spread every imaginable version of her words. The word of something unusual about to happen had traveled as far as Birmingham. Two big city reporters, hastily dispatched, were among the men who crowded for space in the courtroom.

At eight-thirty, Attorney McKye appeared and sat beside J.P. Kinsor. After the usual exchange of pleasantries, both fell silent, each lost in his own thoughts. At eight forty-five, Wash Mabry and Cynthia joined the two men, and the four proceeded to the courthouse, climbed the stairs and took up their respective positions.

The courtroom was truly filled to overflowing. People stood along the walls, sat in windows, some even standing in the hallway and straining to see the proceedings. A buzz of conversation filled the air. Yet there was a sudden and complete silence when the judge emerged from his office. The call to order was unnecessary, though the bailiff evidently didn't think so.

The judge was momentarily silent as he surveyed the courtroom scene. He then repeated the admonition that no outbursts would be tolerated. He emphasized the necessity for silence, especially since Cynthia Kinsor was so handicapped. He then instructed that the defense continue.

"Thank you, your honor. The defense re-calls Cynthia Kinsor."

Cynthia arose, hesitated for a few seconds, and then made her way to the witness chair.

"Mrs. Kinsor, when court recessed yesterday afternoon, you had just finished relating to the court what happened to you on July 23, 1865. You testified that you remembered nothing from then until much later. We have the testimony of Miss Effie Clifton. That testimony accounts for your injuries, your subsequent recovery, and your eventual moving to the home of your husband. I want to ask you if you know of anything else, relevant to your case, that should be revealed today."

Cynthia responded by turning her head toward the jury and tugging on the strings of her bonnet. Still facing the jurors she pulled the bonnet off, revealing a face that, as Birmingham reporter Atticus Mullin later told his editor, "was like something you'd see down the morgue—but it's somehow still living and moving." It was a face whose jawbones were irrevocably out of kilter with the cheekbones, a face whose nose had been flattened and smashed; it was a face whose age lines competed unsuccessfully with livid splashes of scar tissue. You could tell that this had once been the face of a fair-haired young woman with a high forehead and piercing eyes—but what was it now? J.P. brought his hands to his face as the spectators gave a collective gasp; but before they could say much, the judge banged his gavel and shouted "Order! Order! Or I'll clear the courtroom!"

Once the commotion had settled down, Judge Holdbrook fore-stalled Urban Kirksey's objection by asking, in a hard, cold voice: "Mr. McKye, can you explain this sensational display in my court-room? Can you justify what a view of Mrs. Kinsor's unfortunate face has to do with her defense?" McKye struggled to suppress his sense of triumph—after all the judge, no friend of his client's cause, had given him just the opening he wanted. He replied, respectfully but clearly, that he "just wanted the *gentlemen* of the jury to see what Cynthia Kinsor has to live with every day." At which His Honor instructed the jurors "not to take into consideration what they had just seen of the accused's face"—after which juror Micah Jordan looked at his hands and frowned.

Told by Judge Holdbrook to continue, McKye asked Cynthia to put her bonnet back on, and remarked: "Now, I am about to ask you some questions, the answers to which are of utmost importance to your defense."

Having built up drama with his "phraseology," McKye looked briefly at the paper in his hand. He then looked at the jury, from there to the prosecutor, and then to the judge. His eyes came to rest on the witness. She looked back steadily; and he, now irrevocably committed to his strategy, commenced the final move of the de-fense.

"I now ask you when you first remembered what had happened to you."

"I remembered that night as soon as I was good awake; as soon as I was back 'at myself; sometime in the spring of '66. I can't tell exactly."

"Can you tell the court how you felt once you had recalled the events of July 1865?"

"I was fearful—afraid they'd hear I was alive and kill me."

"Did you tell your husband about your fears, and if so, did you tell him the names of your attackers?"

"No. Not 'til recently." Once more her thready voice had gained power.

McKye followed up: "Why not?"

"I was afraid that he'd be hurt or kilt."

"Have you ever told him their names?"

"Not 'til recently."

"Then he cannot be blamed for any part of the crimes you stand charged with committing?"

"No. 'Til th' other day he's been ignorant of what really happened."

"Now Mrs. Kinsor, I ask you, did you kill Alfred Ensor?"

"Yes."

The answer was hesitant, but firm. The spectators were so silent and so determined to hear her testimony that there was no sound in the room. In fact, the silence was now so complete that it could be felt.

Judge Holdbrook broke the silence by asking, "Mrs. Kinsor, I am sure you have been advised by counsel of the consequences of your answer. I now ask you for the record if that is your true answer."

More assertively, she responded: "Yes, sir."

"Very well," said the judge. "Mr. McKye, you may continue."

"Thank you, your honor," replied McKye. "Mrs. Kinsor, you have just admitted to killing Alfred Ensor. I now ask you if you killed Delroy Dobbs."

"Yes."

"And did you attempt to kill Lemuel Emerson?"

"Yes."

"I now ask you why you did not report to the authorities what these three men had done."

"At that time, I felt nobody'd believe me."

"Why not?"

"From the time my family moved here from Ohio, we never really fit in. My family was Union folk, and though there was many natives of the county who b'lieved the same, we outsiders was thought to be the real enemy. We was threatened so much, in fact, that we planned to move back to Ohio. Then come the war. The Rebels wouldn't trust us Yankees. Even after the fighting stopped, outside, it kept on here. In this county." She stopped, her voice giving out, her eyes moving between McKye and her husband.

"But why kill these men, after so long a time?"

"Well," she gathered herself up, then spoke: "I chanced to see 'em, at times, for a long while. At first I wouldn't admit who they was. I didn't do nothin'—didn't think about doin' nothin'—'til I was sure who they was. But by that time, I worried that they'd reco'nized me, and might come back to harm J.P. Still I waited; then each of 'em giv' me the chance I needed."

"Your honor, I have no further questions for this witness," said McKye, rather gently.

Urban Kirksey rose eagerly to his feet, still with the expression that he had worn for the last few minutes: that of a man stunned by good fortune but determined to take advantage of it. He cleared his throat; cleared it again. Advancing on the witness stand, he asked: "So you admit to the treacherous killing of two men, and the attempt to kill a third?"

"Yes," came the answer from within the depths of Cynthia Kinsor's bonneted face, so softly that only Kirksey and the judge could hear her.

"Let the record show," said Kirksey to the courtroom at large, "that the accused has answered in the affirmative." Now the joy that filled his whole being drove him toward concluding with a flourish, an embellishment. It is a self-indulgence common enough among country prosecutors, who must (after all) run for office. Kirksey raised his voice a notch or two, looking sternly at the veiled figure on the witness stand, and asked: "You admit to doing these deeds by stealth, by premeditation, in coldness of blood?"

Then, before she could answer, he took a false step. The adrenalin pumping in his veins, he violated the first, simple rule of cross-examination: *Never ask a question if you're not pretty much sure of the answer.* It was a rule that Kirksey had never quite mastered; his inability to follow it was one of the things that had made him what he was. Now he added, ticking his points off on his fingers: "You planned these deeds without thought of the wives—children—grandchildren—who loved these men, needed them, and will miss them?"

Cynthia answered, her hoarse voice just loud enough for the jury to hear: "The Bible says: 'An eye for an eye.'"

Kirksey acted as if he hadn't heard her. He asked, somewhat contemptuously, if she could repeat herself.

"'An eye for an eye,'" she intoned, with more breath behind the answer. Then she continued, her voice taking on the ruined power with which she had recently described the events of July 23, 1865: "At least I didn't kill their kinfolk."

Leaning forward, the jurors' faces revealed a variety of emotions at this double dose of Old Testament and blood-feud. Kirksey turned from the witness and said, abruptly: "No more questions, your honor; the people are done with this witness."

"And not a moment too soon," thought Judge Holdbrook. Looking over at McKye, he inquired if the defense would be changing its plea to that of "guilty."

"Not in the least," your honor, the attorney responded. "Mrs. Kinsor asserts that two-score years ago these men, by their savagery, passed sentences of death upon themselves."

Judge Holdbrook took a long drink from his water glass, deliberately cleaned his glasses, and asked Urban Kirksey if he were ready for his closing argument. Nodding affirmatively, Kirksey strode rapidly over to the jurors, a strange gleam in his eyes, and began rather abruptly:

"Cynthia Kinsor has admitted in open court to killing two men and attempting to kill a third. Whatever her reasons, she had no right to do that. Mr. McKye speaks of 'truths.' But in a court of law, the facts come first. The facts are that Mrs. Kinsor committed the acts she was charged with doing; she killed with malice aforethought. You gentlemen have been patient as the defense spun its tales of the War Between the States. We are sad for the sufferings of that war; but this is a new era, a different time. You may choose to be sympathetic to Mrs. Kinsor—whether or not you believe all of her stories, and those of her common-law husband. Still, you have no choice but to convict." And he sat down. This was one speech that he hadn't spoiled by saying too much!

Judge Holdbrook asked Ambrose McKye if he were ready for his closing argument. McKye briefly assented, stood up, and walked, buttoning his suit coat, over to the jurors. He looked at them, and in a tone both solemn and conversational, began:

"Most of us fear, almost more than anything else, the prospect of being shut up in prison. That is the punishment my learned opponent would ask you to inflict on Cynthia Kinsor, the self-admitted killer of two men. But you, who have heard the testimony in this case, will understand that the state cannot imprison Mrs. Kinsor—not in the true sense. Since that dreadful night in 1865 she has *been* a prisoner in her mind, in her spirit. You see it embodied in her self-concealing bonnet. You hear it in her faltering voice. Her actions, however misguided, were those of a person seeking to balance accounts; to pay back a debt of blood; to lay the ghosts that have haunted her days and especially her nights. I can only ask that you interpret the truths you have witnessed here in such a way that Cynthia Kinsor may have at least a glimpse of freedom." He sat down.

Silence settled in upon the courtroom. Judge Holdbrook ignored it, taking another sip of water—consulting, then adjusting, his watch. He began speaking, looking only at the jury, in the tone of one who has no doubt that he will be heard and obeyed.

"The people's attorney," he said, "has implied that truth does not enter into legal proceedings. But I, when we opened this trial, noted that law was relentless in the pursuit of truth; and it seems that we have discovered several truths in the course of these proceedings. Our task was to discover whether Cynthia Kinsor is a murderess. Of this there is no longer any doubt; and I hereby charge you that you must convict her of the crimes for which she stands accused. Rest assured that the state will not send her to the gallows. Even if this were the custom in Alabama, I would not be willing to apply that penalty. Jurors, you may retire and consider your verdict. Court is in recess for the duration of your consideration."

26
Verdicts

The bailiff escorted the jurors out of the courtroom. The judge went to his chambers. Wash Mabry rose to escort the Kinsors and lawyer McKye to a waiting room on the first floor. As he did so he cast a long look at Lemuel Emerson. That old man had risen uncertainly to his feet, and was glancing from side to side.

As the inevitable hum of talking broke out, Emerson tottered through the crowd, pursued by one of the Birmingham scribes. The other, a lanky man in a gray three-piece suit, briefly addressed Wash Mabry. "Sheriff," he said, "I'm Atticus Mullins of the *Age-Herald*, and I'd like to talk to Mr. and Mrs. Kinsor." He paused expectantly.

Mabry was just wrinkling up his face to respond when yells, oaths, screams, and a loud report sounded from the stairwell. Rapidly for his size and age, the sheriff made his way across the room to the stairs, at the bottom of which he found the crumpled body of Lemuel Emerson. It was covered with blood, brains and bone fragments that were the result—as men of the crowd all said at once—

of his having jerked a pistol from beneath his jacket and shot himself in the head. The other reporter was sprawled on the stairs near the body, stains covering the front of his blue serge suit. "Rufus Rhodes of the *Birmingham News*, Sheriff," gasped the latter, who was having trouble catching his breath. "That fool"—looking at the body—"drew on me almost as soon as I began askin' him questions." He stopped, still wheezing, fumbling with his pocket notebook, and added, as if writing it down: "Then he turned his pistol on himself!"

Atticus Mullins appeared at the top of the stairs and spoke to his fellow scribe: "Come on Rufe, let's get you cleaned up while I find a telephone." Mabry nodded agreement, adding that he had some questions for the blood-stained reporter; meanwhile he was mentally selecting reliable witnesses from among the stairwell crowd. He then methodically took care of summoning Dr. Starkie, the town's overburdened coroner, to deal with the body, notifying Judge Holdbrook, and steering the Kinsors into a place free of bloodstains. There was no time—yet—to clean up the stairwell. That was not a problem for the citizens of Midville, many of whom were equally anxious to talk about the trial and to see where old Lem Emerson had blown his brains out.

In the jury room, in the courtroom and the courthouse corridors, time slowed—and slowed again. A few spectators left their seats; these were immediately taken by persons who had stood at the back of the courtroom. As minutes stretched into hours, the crowds fidgeted, McKye allowed himself to smile a bit, and the Kinsors kept their companionable silence. Wash Mabry did not change his expression. Nor, in his chambers, did Judge Holdbrook. What Urban Kirksey was undergoing as he paced his office, no one witnessed. But his state of mind could be inferred from the *rictus* that seized control of his face when the bailiff made his rounds declaring: "The jury's coming in."

As the jurors filed back into their chairs, the courtroom audience became hushed, and craned their necks looking for some hint of what the verdict might be. Testimony during the trial had seemed to demand a guilty verdict. But as Atticus Mullins whispered to a now-refurbished Rufus Rhodes, "You can never tell what a jury panel will do."

After the jurymen were seated, Judge Holdbrook made his appearance, heralded as always by his bailiff. Seating himself quickly, the judge gazed upon the twelve men good and true of the jury. Had he expressed an opinion, he probably would have agreed with the big city reporter. Finally he turned toward Harold Hollingsworth, who was seated in the chair given over to the jury foreman: "Mr. Foreman, has the jury reached a verdict?"

"We have, your honor," said the latter, standing up.

"Please stand," said the judge in the direction of Cynthia Kinsor, J.P. Kinsor, and Ambrose McKye. Then, to Hollingsworth: "What do you find?"

The foreman faced the defense table, and read clearly but mechanically: "We, the jury, find the defendant guilty as charged." Pausing slightly, he turned to face Judge Holdbrook and said slowly and very firmly: "*And we recommend that she be sentenced to time served, and that she be released from custody as of today.*"

Judge Holdbrook banged his gavel as the courtroom erupted in a cacophony of voices. "There will be order in this court," he shouted. "Any further outbursts and I'll clear the court!" A few more bangs of the gavel, and the room grew quiet again. He resumed his colloquy with the jury. "The court thanks each and all jurors for your service to the community. You have been a most attentive and conscientious panel, and the court will take your recommendations under consideration. You are hereby dismissed from your duties."

The jurymen stayed in their seats as Holdbrook looked down at his notes. He looked up and fixed his gaze on Cynthia and J.P. Kinsor. Free or jail? Urban Kirksey was standing up, but the judge waved him back into his seat. He thought to himself that he could delay the proceedings; he could set a date for sentencing. Either way—now or later—free or jail—he would have his doubts. Either way he would anger neighbors and kin: a bad thing, for he was an elected official. Which verdict would anger the fewest and please the most? Free or jail? Just or unjust? He gathered himself, cutting off the internal debate, and spoke:

"Mrs. Kinsor, you have been found guilty of two murders and one attempted murder. These are dreadful crimes. Yet the court has great sympathy for your experiences with those who, on that night so long ago, destroyed your family and left you for dead. Though they did not kill you, you have endured punishments almost unimaginable. I am inclined to doubt whether your revenge, however complete"—he glanced toward the stairwell exit—"will give you the peace you desire." He gazed upward toward the ceiling fans, seemingly lost in a moment of prayer, before continuing, in a loud voice: "But that peace is not our concern at this time. I agree with the jury that you have already been punished for your crimes; and I therefore sentence you to time served. Sheriff Mabry, you will release Mrs. Kinsor from custody."

As an uproar of shouts and cheers broke out, he banged the gavel and declared: "This court is adjourned." Now freed from restraint, several of the watchers rose to their feet and launched a vigorous round of applause, joined eventually by most of the citizens in the room and a number who were still in the passageways—most of whom were unaware of the resentful looks of several spectators. Turning briefly as he ushered the Kinsors out a side entrance, McKye recognized several Triple-S members—Elwin DeJohn,

Ezekiel Vanderhooven, and Jim-Joe Peterson among them, all clapping and grinning.

McKye also saw his learned colleague Urban Kirksey, still standing at the prosecution table. Two powerful feelings were struggling for mastery of the District Attorney's face. The first was a kind of flummoxed joy: "I've done it!" he couldn't help thinking over and over. The second was resentment: that Judge Holdbrook had taken it upon himself to spoil the full measure of this triumph. Already Kirksey was thinking how to make political hay of the Kinsor verdict.

Among those who were *not* clapping was the Rev. Mike Wycliffe Amos. As he gazed upon the company of the damned (thinking ahead to his next sermon), he was accosted by Ansel Deavors, who had snagged a seat nearby during the jury's deliberation. The two men had a conversation whose exchanges were masked by the sounds of celebration. At the end of it, Rev. Mike strode away, prim and tightlipped. Deavors hesitated for a moment before stalking out; this time he didn't bother to conceal his smile.

27

An Interlude of Freedom

The old couple trudged slowly toward Ambrose McKye's office, moving in a daze marked by alternating waves of happiness and fatigue. As they approached they saw a smart delivery wagon drawn up before the door. J.P. recognized the buckskin hitched to the post as a strong, tractable horse, Jeff Jordan's best. As they crossed the street, a dapper figure emerged from behind the van, a grey-headed black man wearing a gray suit and black Stetson hat. He took off his hat and waved them across, saying: "Mr. and Mrs. Kinsor, so pleasant to see you on such a fine day!"

J.P., whose memory had been jogged more than once in recent months, had no difficulty in placing the man's features, however they had aged. It was a face he'd kept safe in memory—belonging to a man he'd seen every day during an eternity of days, that drawn-out monument of time they had shared during their youth—the last, violent days of the Army of Northern Virginia. "Hello, Nate," he said, adding: "I hope you're bringing good news from Farmville." Then, amused by one of the memories passing in review in his mind, J.P. asked: "How'd you ever get holt of my pistol?" Nate laughed, and said: "I was "carrying some of those Union rations back to Mr. Alfred, when I saw the big tent where they'd stowed the Rebel weapons. I took a look—and there was your Colt! The Yankees had borrowed it; I decided to borrow it back. Who wants to travel without an argument to hand?" J.P. laughed, then turned toward Cynthia and McKye, quickly introducing them to Nate Courtney, "My best friend's servant back from wartime."

It was quickly decided that Nate should drive the Kinsors home, based on an arrangement he had previously made with Ed Raye. "I've got comfortable seats fixed up in the back of this vehicle. You'll be out of the wind and out of sight of those reporters." In this Nate was thinking along the same lines as Sheriff Mabry, who had cornered Messrs. Mullins and Rhodes with the promise of a post-trial interview and "exclusive" information on old man Emerson's suicide. After a few words with Ambrose McKye, Cynthia and J.P. climbed in. Nate chirruped the buckskin; they stopped only at Wash Mabry's house, where Nate retrieved Cynthia's travel kit. For a little more than an hour, they drove the rutted way north to Eau Clair Springs.

During the trip, they talked. Nate had learned a good deal about the Kinsors from the letters that Alfred Courtney had shown him. Ed Raye, whose hair Nate had cut just before the trial, had filled in the gaps once he learned Nate's history. And as for Nate himself: "I always wanted to see the country," he told the Kinsors. "That's one thing that a man of my color couldn't do freely—before. And since my barberin' skills have gotten to be first-rate, I found that I could make money in the crossroads towns." Over the last few years he had stopped two or three times in Midville. He had hoped to connect with J.P. but was uncertain how to search beyond the town; and he was shy about asking too many questions. "I'm a mite surprised," J.P. interjected, "with that nice suit and those fancy chromos, that you didn't have some trouble anyway." Nate nodded, but said: "I talk mighty humble to customers; and besides, folks expect barbers to look natty. Plus, they just naturally love those signs."

Steering around a mudhole, Nate added: "I'm always careful not to stay anyplace too long." By chance, as it developed, Nate had been in Rome, Georgia late in November, where one of his customers told him of an unusual court case, a triple-poisoning affair, that was about to be tried just across the Alabama line in Midville. Soon after he had telegraphed to Alfred Courtney, who wired that he could not come himself, at least not in time—but begged Nate to help any way he could. "So I asked Mr. Jeff Jordan for directions. I decided to trust *him*, and found out"—this with a wry laugh—"that I could've asked him anything all along," As they pulled up to the Kinsor place, they saw Ed Raye on the front porch. Nate returned his wave, and told the Kinsors: "Mr. Ed has been watching over the place."

Once the Kinsors had exchanged greetings with Ed Raye—and Cynthia had murmured raspy greetings to her several dogs and cats—they moved about the house checking its contents and delighting in the simple familiarities of home. Soon they were joined by Ambrose McKye and Delnora—who, having managed to prepare several of her specialties, had packed them securely in McKye's buggy. While supper was warming in the wood-burning stove, Cynthia asked Delnora and Nate to eat with the rest of the guests. Both refused politely but firmly—Nate no less firmly than Delnora, who said: "No, thank you, Ma'am. Miss Chrissy wouldn't like to hear about it." Thus this group of celebratory folks, whose ties were so closely bound, preserved the region's self-defeating etiquette. The white folks sat down to their feast-in-the-wilderness around the kitchen table, while Nate and Delnora obeyed the racial code and dined on the back gallery.

To people accustomed to plain fare, Delnora's cooking always seemed to be a kind of culinary matinee. For a brief time it transported them to a place where race and class—or crime and punishment—had no place. Afterwards, J.P., Nate, and Ed Raye moved to the front porch to smoke while Cynthia and Delnora put up leftovers in the pie safe. Lawyer McKye washed the dishes—a thing he sometimes did for Delnora at home. Shortly thereafter, the shadows beginning to lengthen, the two of them left for town.

28

Prelude to Violence

As supper settled and the dishes dried, they all—Cynthia, J.P., Nate, and Ed Raye—sat on the front porch to watch the sun set over the Eau Claire oaks. As the evening faded to a wisteria shade, two figures came on horseback down the road from town. Even in the dim light, J.P. recognized them as Sheriff Mabry and Deputy Bankston. For a moment he feared that they had come to re-arrest Cynthia; on instinct he came down into the yard to meet them. Mabry shook hands with J.P. and remarked that he had passed lawyer McKye on the way. Then he delivered his bad news in a clear, raised voice: "Fred, here, has told me that there may be an attack on your house tonight or early tomorrow morning. Evidently, the Whitecappers have decided that you and Mrs. Kinsor are an affront to the community!"

"I thought it had all been decided in court!" burst out J.P. Then more quietly: "We're not bothering nobody." His face in the twilight was a study of imperfectly repressed feelings.

"Some people take their pleasure out in anger," said Mabry. "It makes them feel good when they're filled to the brim with hate. Best of all when they injure those who can't fight back. In the dark, in an ambush, they're big men! And they always think that they're getting away with it."

"It won't go easy this time," J.P. said coldly, and like the old soldier he was, he limped back up the steps to inspect his weapons. Before he entered the house he spoke with Raye, who sought out his mule and headed home to get his squirrel rifle. Nate patted his hip pocket and muttered: "Always an argument to hand."

"I'll leave Fred with you tonight," Mabry told the assembly. "I'll come back when I can, but right now I need to talk to the Rev. Mike—I sent for him today, but he didn't come. If I can find him, he might be able to stop this before it starts." Turning his horse toward the road he mounted and rode purposefully back toward town.

Clouds flowed in over most of the sky. There was little or no moon. Darkness deepened to the east. Even under the Eau Claire oaks the last of twilight frustrated "all but those who boasted superior nocturnal oculation"—that's how the just-returned Ed Raye put it, in a whispered comment to Cynthia. They were stationed in the center of the house, well back in the dogtrot. Nate with his pistol was on the back porch. J.P. and Deputy Bankston were out front. They burned no lights. Cynthia's pack of dogs were tucked away, to their canine bemusement, in the couple's sitting room.

Sometime after midnight a faint blur of light appeared at some little distance down the Midville road. Bankston crept out to the roadway; in a few minutes he saw a line of mounted men headed by one carrying a lantern. Stopping less than a hundred yard's walk from the Kinsors' dooryard, they dismounted, tied their horses to bushes and fenceposts. Several dark figures approached the light-bearer; from his lantern they ignited torches they had carried from

Ansel Deavors' barn. The blaze of illumination revealed to Bankston that the men were wearing flour bags over their heads with cut-outs for eyes.

In response to the roadside torches, a minute blur of light—then another, brighter, ablaze—shone forth at the tree line behind the Kinsor place. These side-lights caught Bankston's eye. He walked carefully from his spy post to the Kinsors' steps, told J.P. what he had seen, and whispered: "Make sure everybody knows." J.P. spoke softly to Ed and Cynthia; the former moved toward Nate's post. Then J.P. said: "Those fools think they'll catch us sleeping." Bankston took up a post before the bushes to J.P.'s left, saying to nobody in particular: "Looks like Sheriff Mabry's mission has failed."

29

Behind the House

Nate watched two Whitecappers advance on foot toward the back porch and well-yard of the Kinsor Place. "Br'er Lantern," he noted to himself, "has a shotgun draped over his arm." He couldn't see how the torch-man was armed. Thinking of the shotgun, he hissed "Git down, git back!" to Ed and Cynthia, who huddled together in one of the doorways opening off the dogtrot. By the time the marauders were within a few yards of the house, Nate was crouched off to his own left, deep in the shadows.

As the two men drew close, the sound of someone cursing—the voice of their leader—came from the front yard. The Lantern man took no special notice; but when he was close enough to funnel buckshot down the dogtrot, he put down his light, raised his weapon, and cheerfully announced: "Here's something to wake up the old folks." He fired both barrels, a thunderous noise that partially covered the report of Nate's pistol.

Hit square in the gut with a .44 caliber slug, Lantern man fell back gasping and crying and clutching his middle. Torch-bearer looked about wildly, then flung his torch toward the porch. It missed; in fact it fell into a zinc tub full of drinking water for the dogs. Determined to see something burn, he grasped the lantern and tossed it onto the porch. Glass broke and kerosene spilled, but just as it started to ignite Nate jumped, grabbed the handle, and hurled the flaming mass back onto the would-be arsonist. Nate's right hand was singed, but he had the pleasure of watching the Whitecapper, his shirt and flour bag on fire, run for the woods screaming and stripping off his clothing—a vanishing stream of light.

Nate jumped into the yard and plunged his hand—smarting good and proper—into the zinc tub. As he calmed down, he heard a stolid voice—Ed Raye's—cursing in the way men used to curse when brought back to camp wounded but not incapacitated. Ever curious, Ed Raye had not kept his head fully covered; he was lucky to have been hit by only two of the buckshot. One of them grazed his left cheek; the other took a chunk off his left ear. He bled briefly but profusely.

Momentarily the cursing resumed in the front door-yard. Nate crept toward the dogtrot but kept to his post. An ex-slave, he had received his military training second hand; but as a veteran of Petersburg he knew how to serve the twin gods of duty and survival. Instantly he heard tempestuous baying that started in the dogtrot and receded toward the road. Cynthia had quieted her dogs when she sequestered them. Now she had loosed them on the Whitecappers.

30
The Front Yard and Beyond

In the minutes before the events described above, seven torch-bearing Whitecappers moved to the edge of the Kinsors' front yard, following their leader. Light-blinded by their torches, they could not yet see Fred Bankston's post to the right of the house, or J.P. on the porch itself.

To the Whitecappers, the house seemed completely dark and silent; still, they hung back, fearing an ambush. Not so their leader, who approached the Kinsor place on a diagonal line. Soon enough, he made out Bankston's form in his lantern light; coming closer, he fixed his sight on the deputy's double-barreled shotgun, for the moment pointed at the ground.

This was not the reception he had expected, but he put on a brave face. "Depitty Bankston," he said, keeping his voice low, "Pleasure to see you! You'd best be gittin' along back home. We're here to pay a social call on J.P. and Cynthia."

Bankston replied: "Ansel Deavors, you'd best take that flour bag off your face—I know your voice too well. Heard you drunk and cryin' for your momma in the cells at Midville—too often! You 'n your scared buddies over yonder are the ones who need to be off home." Bankston shifted the shotgun, raising it slightly.

Deavors responded: "Naw, you ain't goin' to shoot me—Sheriff Mabry will have told you that much. I'm one of his partic'lar pets. He won't give up on me until I'm truly re-formed." He looked around, voice and temper rising: "We're here to git ol' Kinsor and that bitch-freak. They've been floutin' the Laws of God these many years. Rev. Mike says that God is patient but vengeful. Now He's goin' to see 'em cut down. We're the Reapers! Where are those cowards? Are they here?"

At this point, J.P. descended the porch's dark steps, walking into his front yard. He stood still, his arms crossed, a few feet from Deavors. The latter unleashed a torrent of profanity at J.P.'s face and was just starting to signal his followers forward when the shotgun blast came roaring down the dogtrot, rattling off the walls and floor and zipping into the bushes that lined the roadway. Deavors flinched, but not J.P—even though he was stung by a ricocheting pellet. Bankston calmly brought his shotgun level. Still in his white-cap, Deavors resumed his rant as wails came from the back yard. A moment later, the sound of baying dogs—a wall of sound—split the night air.

Cynthia had stepped out into the dogtrot. Holding the door open and pointing toward the road, she gave her dogs her own, personal find-it-and-kill-it signal. Pack-leader Bingley, knowing full well that the house was under attack, started an angry music that was magnified by the long hollow space. He tore down the front steps past his master, drawn by the torch lights and the scent of fear; he was followed by the Kinsor hounds, the shepherd, and several terriers, all headed straight toward the torch-bearing White-cappers. These masked avengers threw down torches and ran for the horses, some getting off wild pistol shots. How many of them were bitten, and how badly, were subjects of Midville speculation for years to come.

Cynthia briefly held back guard dog Lady, pointing her toward her master's side. Instantly sizing up Deavors, she launched herself at his right leg, her jaws almost meeting in the muscles just above his knee. Deavors kept his footing by a miracle, dropped the lantern, and tugged at the pistol he carried in his hip pocket; it discharged as he pulled it free. Simultaneously, J.P. extended his right hand and fired a round from his small Colt into Deavors' face. Deavors fell heavily, twitched once and was still. J.P. called Lady off, muttering to himself: "Bastard made me break my promise."

Deputy Bankston, whose stance through these brief seconds had been one of "masterly inactivity," prodded the dead man with the toe of his boot. "Well, Ansel," he said, "I reckon that you are *truly* re-formed."

Moving to the back yard via the dogtrot, Bankston assessed Ed Raye's condition and promised to send for Dr. Jim-Joe as soon as possible. He advised Nate to put away his pistol, saying: "If it's all the same with you, I'll claim credit for shooting"—he pulled the hood from the head of the Lantern man, now silent—"Bobby Lee Plunkett here." Then, to the corpse: "Bit off one too many, huh, Bobby?"

Nate returned his "argument" to his hip pocket, saying: "Happy to avoid the Race Question tonight, and most nights."

31
One Month Later: January 1908

Thus was formed an informal conspiracy, devoted to perfecting one particular version of events. Fred Bankston laid out the story: That it had been he who, guarding the Kinsors' back yard, had killed Bobby Lee Plunkett after Plunkett fired his shotgun. Bankston said that he had watched Plunkett's unknown comrade run back into the woods, all the while he, Bankston, was easing around to the front of the house. There Bankston had seen Deavors fire his pistol, before J.P. returned fire; the deputy was emphatic that J.P.'s response came in self-defense.

He further observed that Deavors' comrades had run away when they realized that the dogs were coming after them. In Bankston's version, Nate was at the Kinsors' house only to cut J.P.'s hair and had not taken any part in the fighting. Ed Raye was merely a concerned neighbor, a victim of the Whitecappers' reckless violence. The deputy admitted that Cynthia had loosed the dogs at the very end of the business. Otherwise she had been hidden inside the house.

The story stood up well on the two occasions it was tested. First, a coroner's jury concluded that the dead men had met their deaths during a cowardly midnight attack on an occupied dwelling; the jurors, all neighbors of Ed Raye, declared that both dead men were justifiably killed. Second, the parties had to face a grand jury convened by Urban Kirksey shortly after the New Year. Kirksey was hoping to indict J.P. for manslaughter; but the grand jurors, after hearing Bankston's eyewitness account of Deavors' death, refused to bring in a true bill. Sheriff Mabry had asked the prosecutor to subpoena the Rev. Mike W. Amos. Kirksey refused, saying that he had no intention of inconveniencing a prominent man of the cloth.

Two days after the grand jury broke up, a still-bandaged Ed Raye had driven Nate to the train station in Gadsden, accompanied by Deputy Bankston on horseback. Before he got aboard the Negro car of the northbound train, Nate looked Bankston in the eye and thanked him for "shooting Mr. Plunkett so fortuitously."

Bankston replied: "You've been spending too much time around Ed Raye."

Earlier, as he had stowed his luggage and signs aboard Raye's wagon, Nate had said his goodbyes to J.P. and Cynthia. He and J.P. had exchanged a firm embrace without saying anything. Then Nate remarked: "I hope that we've just won the *last* battle of the Army of Northern Virginia"—which brought forth from J.P. one of his rare laughs.

After Nate's safe departure, an impromptu meeting of the Triple-S Society had convened at the Kinsor place. Present were Sheriff Mabry, Lawyer McKye, Dr. Jim-Joe Peterson, Judge Elwin DeJohn, and Ed Raye. All were agreed that J.P. and Cynthia should seize the moment—farm duties being light in the dead of winter— to visit March and his family in Texas. Members of the society, said McKye, would take up a collection for round-trip tickets. "Enjoy yourselves and get to know your grandchildren," he said. "You can pay us back when and how you choose." Ed Raye added: "I'll keep my optics on your homeplace and look after your animal lodgers. Stay a couple of months—avoid the vicissitudes of the winter, and keep shy of our Whitecap friends." The sheriff nodded assent to Raye's last remark, saying: "The attack on your house was completely unacceptable! But we'll try to have that problem solved by the time you get back."

A few days later, J.P. and Cynthia were enjoying their first railway ride on an L&N train that would take them to Birmingham, Montgomery, New Orleans, and on to Texas. As the unfamiliar landscape blurred past their window, Cynthia whispered: "Are we ever going back to Midville?" J.P. patted the return ticket in his bib pocket before saying: "Yes! The spring will come on, the creek will rise, and it will be time for us to tend our garden. Our animals will need us, *and* our neighbors—where else should we be?"

Afterword

Born in 1919, my father was raised on a farm in Cherokee County in northeastern Alabama. He grew up down the road from James Polk Knight, a Confederate veteran crippled in gait but not in spirit, a great storyteller who captured young Paul's imagination. Naturally Paul was also influenced, as he lived the challenging life of a farm boy in Depression-era Alabama, by his father, George Pruitt, and by his father's friends. In the 1890s these men (boys, as they were then) attended the county's leading school, Gaylesville Academy. From that experience they carried away a respect for learning and the life of the mind, and an enduring confidence in each other.

By the time Paul was in his early teens, one of these friends was sheriff of the county; another was probate judge. One was a physician, another a banker; one was the county's most respected lawyer. To the boy's mind they ran the county, and ran it well. As for George Pruitt, he had remained on his family's farm—with some detours into coal mining—and sought to build a modest fortune. He never lost contact with his Gaylesville Academy classmates. Paul overheard many conversations at the courthouse in Centre, at church, at the bank, or at the supply store.

The life of the mind may not have figured to any great extent in these chance meetings, but Paul did enjoy talking with another neighbor, Ed Ray, his father's kinsman. Ed was a farmer and part-time moonshiner whose consistent goal was to work less and read more. Here was a man who loved words, subscribed to several newspapers and magazines, and read an encyclopedia for pleasure. What was more, he had no higher ambition. His life, to a teenaged boy, must have seemed almost perfect.

Sitting at the feet of J.P. Knight, Paul derived an enduring sympathy for heroism in a losing cause. Observing George Pruitt and his classmates, Paul saw public business conducted in a collegial manner. In Ed Ray he found a man who valued learning above bales of cotton. Once he sat down to write his novel, he had a ready-made cast of characters who had been running around in his head for decades. How he set them in motion, how he connected them with the complicated, often tragic, history of Alabama and the South—these things you, his readers, have seen.

Paul M. Pruitt, Jr.
Tuscaloosa, Alabama

Visit us at *www.quidprobooks.com*.

www.ingramcontent.com/pod-product-compliance
Lightning Source LLC
Chambersburg PA
CBHW071435260626
47170CB00008B/2721